1

THE NAKED SUN BORE DOWN WITH AN UN-relenting glare causing the line-back dun to be lathered in sweat as it struggled upslope behind an outcropping of boulders. Kenyon reined to a halt and dismounted. He didn't like running the gelding over unfamiliar ground. It was too easy for the animal to break a leg. He also didn't like being chased by anyone, especially five *pistoleros* intent on robbing him. He pulled the Winchester from its scabbard, then stepped back to watch the trail.

A breeze began to pick up, fluttering the golden leaves on the Emory oaks. A ground squirrel's sharp ratcheting call echoed up the draw, and a moment later Kenyon could see dust kicked up by the hooves of five horses. He levered a round into the chamber and waited. A hummingbird zoomed up and checked him over, then left, a dark-headed, green-breasted bullet disappearing over the trees.

The pistoleros had seen his gelding tied to the hitching rail outside a cantina a few miles south of the border. They had entered the saloon and sat at a table, and they had watched him buy a *cerveza* with the only money he had, a twenty-dollar gold piece. They had looked, with covetous eyes, at his ivory-handled Colt .45 and his lever-action Winchester carbine, and they had decided, after some heated discussion, that this gringo was worth robbing. There wouldn't be much to split among five men, but Kenyon knew that border bandits were not known for being particularly bright or choosy.

His knowledge of Spanish had enabled him to understand their plans. He had been aware of the pistoleros the moment they had entered the cantina. He had the ability to read people and to be aware of everything going on around him. It was the result of lessons learned over the years, which had made him a survivor in a land where those who didn't learn didn't live.

As soon as he was outside, he had mounted the dun and taken off at a gallop. Then, as he passed the last building on the street, he turned the gelding toward the hills and nudged him into a dead run. Now, after several miles of running, he had reached the mountain's skirts and the terrain had steepened too abruptly to continue pushing a fast pace. Both he and the dun had had enough.

As the first horseman appeared, Kenyon drew a bead on the man's shoulder. He didn't want to kill any of them unless it was absolutely necessary. When he squeezed off a shot, the pistolero fell from the saddle, and the others quickly dismounted and scattered. In a few moments one of the bandits fired several shots in the general direction of the boulder where Kenyon crouched, while two others scurried out and dragged the injured man behind some rocks.

"Hey, gringo, you *cabrón,* you shoot my brother, so I am going to keel you!" shouted the one Kenyon had heard called Emiliano back in the cantina.

"Why don't you get your brother to the doctor and take your friends with you? Then I won't have to kill *you,*" Kenyon answered.

The wounded man yelled, "I'm going to keel you myself, you cabrón."

He fired two wild shots. The other four spread out in an attempt to surround their prey.

KENYON

QUINT WADE

A SIGNET BOOK

NEW AMERICAN LIBRARY

NAL BOOKS ARE AVAILABLE AT QUANTITY DISCOUNTS WHEN USED TO PROMOTE PRODUCTS OR SERVICES. FOR INFORMATION PLEASE WRITE TO PREMIUM MARKETING DIVISION, NEW AMERICAN LIBRARY, 1633 BROADWAY, NEW YORK, NEW YORK 10019.

PUBLISHER'S NOTE

This book is a work of fiction. Names, characters, places, and incidents either are the product of the author's imagination or are used fictitiously, and any resemblance to actual persons, living or dead, events, or locales is entirely coincidental.

Copyright © 1988 by James Dunwoody and Suzanne Dunwoody

All rights reserved.

SIGNET TRADEMARK REG. U.S. PAT. OFF. AND FOREIGN COUNTRIES
REGISTERED TRADEMARK—MARCA REGISTRADA
HECHO EN CHICAGO. U.S.A.

SIGNET, SIGNET CLASSIC, MENTOR, ONYX, PLUME, MERIDIAN and NAL BOOKS are published by NAL PENGUIN INC., 1633 Broadway, New York, New York 10019

First Printing, July, 1988

1 2 3 4 5 6 7 8 9

PRINTED IN THE UNITED STATES OF AMERICA

SUNDAY SHOWDOWN

Kenyon showed up as scheduled, on the sun-drenched dirt strip that served as the town's main street. He saw the cattle king Ben Terrell waiting for him, and remembered how Terrell had vowed to kill him. Terrell's hired hand, Shorty, was also there and Kenyon knew that Shorty, too, wanted him dead. But the most important man waiting was E. J. Wingate. As Kenyon stared at the man, he recalled the grisly fate of all the men Wingate had outdrawn and outshot throughout the West.

Wingate smiled coldly. "Well, Kenyon, I'm mighty pleased to see you here. A man should learn to stand up and take his lumps."

And without another word, Wingate separated himself from the others and stepped into the street. His fingers rested on the sides of his holsters, as he announced: "Okay, Kenyon, make your move."

And Kenyon knew it was now or never. . . .

W4X
① SIGNET (0451)

ROUGH RIDERS

- [ ] **THE HIGHBINDERS by F.M. Parker.** They left him for dead ... and now it was his turn to kill. A vicious gang of outlaws were out for miner's gold and young Tom Galletin stood alone against the killing crew ... until he found an ally named Pak Ho. Together they had to cut down all the odds against them ... with Galletin's flaming Colt .45 and Pak Ho's razor-sharp, double edged sword. (155742—$2.95)

- [ ] **THE RAWHIDERS by Ray Hogan.** Forced outside the law, Matt Buckman had to shoot his way back in. Rescued from the savage Kiowas by four men who appeared suddenly to save him, Matt Buckman felt responsible for the death of one and vowed to ride in his place. Soon he discovered that filling the dead man's boots would not be easy ... he was riding with a crew of killers ... killers he owed his life to.... (143922—$2.75)

- [ ] **COLTER by Quint Wade.** Colter's brother was gunned down in a hell-hole Arizona town, and nothing was going to stop Colter from finding his killer ... not the hired guns who left him for dead, not the sheriff who told him to clear out, not even the cold-as-steel cattle baron who owned everyone in town. But lots of men were going to stop his bullets as he blazed a trail to the truth.... (151925—$2.75)

- [ ] **KENYON by Quint Wade.** Kenyon had his work cut out for him. There was his greenhorn sidekick who couldn't stay out of trouble. There were the widows putting their lives on the line to save their land. There was a land-grabbing cattle king and his cutthroat crew. And then there was Wingate, the most feared gunfighter in the West, who was in town to cut Kenyon down.... (154053—$2.75)

- [ ] **THE KINCAIDS by Matt Braun.** They tamed an untamed land—but not the passions raging within them. Over three generations and tens of thousands of Western wilderness acres, theirs was the kingdom, the power, and the glory of the American dream.... (153693—$4.50)

*Prices slightly higher in Canada.

Buy them at your local bookstore or use this convenient coupon for ordering.

NEW AMERICAN LIBRARY
P.O. Box 999, Bergenfield, New Jersey 07621

Please send me the books I have checked above. I am enclosing $_____
(please add $1.00 to this order to cover postage and handling). Send check or money order—no cash or C.O.D.'s. Prices and numbers are subject to change without notice.

Name_____

Address_____

City _____ State _____ Zip Code _____

Allow 4-6 weeks for delivery.
This offer is subject to withdrawal without notice.

Kenyon knew that the wounded man would not be a threat and that his shouting and his shooting were just a show of macho. The other four, however, were definitely something to contend with. Two of them came toward him from the left side, one from the right, and one directly up the center. Since the two on his left were moving faster, he concentrated his attention on them. One was twenty feet or so ahead of the other, so Kenyon drew a bead on the bandito's legs and fired. The man went down and screamed as he grabbed his knee, part of which had been blown away.

The other three stopped moving, uncertain as to what they should do now that two of their party were down.

They decided to discuss the situation without exposing themselves to Kenyon's rifle. While they were talking back and forth across the small ravine that led up to the boulders, Kenyon picked up a large rock and rolled it down through the brush to the bottom of the draw. The pistoleros instantly opened up a barrage of shots at what they were certain was the gringo trying to escape. The sound of ricocheting lead filled the air for a few seconds until one of them yelled.

"Ai, chingada!" That was followed by a low moan.

Kenyon grinned. In the crossfire, one of the thieves had shot the other.

"Que pasó?" the one in the middle asked in a hoarse whisper.

"Le echaron un balazo, burro!" Emiliano grumbled, his voice growing in volume as he bent over the man who had been shot.

Kenyon got a sight on the middle man's arm and squeezed the trigger. The bandit squealed and dropped his gun.

Emiliano made a quick mental check and decided that four down and one to go didn't look too good, especially since he was the one to go. His brother's call from down below quickly convinced him that his decision to quit was a good one.

"Olvida el gringo, Emiliano. Necesito un médico."

"Bueno, Ramon," Emiliano answered. Then turning his attention once more to Kenyon he yelled.

"You are lucky, gringo. We have decided not to keel you."

Kenyon waited until the injured men had moved down the hill toward their horses. Then he mounted up and headed the dun toward Arizona Territory.

2

THE CLOUDS THAT SCRAPED THE WORN FACE of the mountains were without a trace of yesterday's gray. They held no promised dropping of rain as they crossed the dry desert floor, and therefore, Riley did not get his hopes up as he had done yesterday and the day before. The winter had been a strange one. Snow had come down into the valley on at least four different occasions since Christmas. Now many of the old-timers were predicting a wet spring, which would be about as strange as the winter that had just finished, for southern Arizona Territory rarely had rain until the summer months. Riley had gone along with those predictions even to the point of betting Mr. Harrison down at the saloon that today would be the day it rained. He studied the clouds for a moment. "Heckfire, them thangs ain't even gonna last ten minutes," he grumbled.

The bet wasn't for money, of course, but he knew Mr. Harrison would exact a heavy price in the ribbing that was sure to come.

During their half-minute passage, the clouds' shadows covered the ghostlike skeletons of the Arizona sycamore. The accompanying breeze fluttered the new spring growth of leaves on limbs that had remained stripped of foliage during the winter. Then, as the clouds began to dissipate from the rising waves of heated air, Riley shook his head. "I lost again."

Scratching his bony bottom through a thin pair of badly stained Levi's, he went back inside the small storeroom of Edson's Emporium and pulled on his boots.

Mr. Edson let Riley sleep in the storeroom partly because Edson had replaced the lock at least half a dozen times only to find it broken by some drunk before the week was out. Also, Riley had offered to sweep out the store six days a week in exchange for the use of the shed and an occasional can of food.

As Riley emerged and stretched, he could hear the voices of churchgoers on their way to hear the Reverend Mr. Hockworth deliver his fiery sermon on the evils of the demon whiskey. Riley had always enjoyed going to church when his mother was alive, at least up to the time he was sixteen. That was a little over a year ago. He hadn't lost the faith. He still prayed—on occasion. He had just outgrown his clothes, and with his mother being ill for so long, they couldn't afford new clothes and medicine too. When she first got sick, he had tried to work the farm by himself, but it hadn't been enough. She had to stay in bed most of the time. When the bank foreclosed on their farm and took everything, she lost the will to continue and died two days later. Riley had managed to keep his pinto filly and his saddle, only because he had hidden them from creditors. That was all he had in the world.

He smiled as he headed down behind the buildings to Harrison's saloon. Since it was Sunday, he didn't have to sweep Edson's store, but he did have to clean Harrison's saloon. The place was usually a mess after all the Saturday night drinking and brawling that went on, and Harrison always gave Riley a dollar for sweeping it up, but that included washing and polishing all of the brass spittoons.

Riley figured Mr. Harrison would start chiding him about their bet on the weather as soon as he got there, but Harrison didn't. He sat trying to pinch off bits of wood from the stub of a pencil he was using so he could free the lead and get the damned thing to make a mark on the paper. After all, he couldn't tally up last night's receipts without using something to add up the sum with. As he pried hard with his thumbnail, it suddenly gave way and bent backwards. "You sonofabitch!" He threw the pencil stub over the bar where it banged into the mirror along the back wall and dropped to the floor. Then he stuck his thumbnail into his mouth.

"What did I do?" Riley asked, pausing to lean on the broom for a moment as he looked up.

"I didn't mean you, kid," Harrison grumbled. "I bent my nail back into the quick on that goddamned stub I was tryin' to write with."

Riley went back to work and was soon daydreaming about the land he was going to own some day.

Harrison studied the young man's methodical movements as he sucked on his wounded thumb. He liked Riley. The boy was a good worker, a hard worker who had just been dealt a bad hand. If that worthless father of his hadn't run off and left Mrs. Riley and the boy in debt, then the bank wouldn't have stripped them of their land with that damned foreclosure. Well, it was really none of his concern. Riley did a good job, and he enjoyed kidding the boy. He'd leave it at that. Now, he'd better get back to those figures and that stub of a pencil again. He shifted his weight on to one cheek and farted, a real thread popper. "Sharpen that for me will you, kid?"

Riley looked up and grinned. "Now that'll take some doin'."

Harrison's brow wrinkled in confusion for a moment. "I mean the pencil for christsake!" he said shaking his head. Then a chuckle started deep down in his chest. By the time it reached the surface, it had volcanic force behind it.

Riley loved to catch Harrison off guard, which didn't happen too often. With a grin still splitting his face, he leaned his broom against the front wall and headed for the back of the bar to find the pencil stub Harrison had thrown there.

The bat-wing doors creaked as the four Hagan brothers entered. Bronco sniffed the air as they stepped to the bar.

"Smells like an outhouse in here. Don't you ever air this place out, Harrison? It stinks!"

"You brought that in with you," Harrison mumbled.

"I'll bet that senorita he's got cookin' for him don't feed him nothin' but them free-holies ever' day," Orville commented with a chuckle.

"You should talk, Orville Hagan. A man that smells as bad as you do would chase a buzzard off a dead wagon. Ain't you never heard of soap?"

"Well . . . hell . . . what . . . you ain't too sweet-smellin' either, old man."

Zeke, Bronco, and Carl laughed at Orville's clumsy retort.

"You'd better not git him ticked off, Orville, or he won't sell us a drank," Bronco said softly.

"That's sure as hell right!" Harrison snapped.

A high-pitched cackle from behind the bar caused the brothers to turn around.

Orville glared at Riley. "What in the hell are you a-chucklin' about, toothpick?"

"I just thought that Mr. Harrison was funny," Riley said.

"Well, who in the hell asked you?" Orville continued.

"You did," Riley answered.

While Orville mulled over what Riley had said, Zeke stepped in.

"Ain't you that skinny little fart that cleans up Edson's store?"

"Yeah, I sweep it out, but I ain't no little fart."

"Here," Zeke said, flipping a fifty-cent piece into a spittoon. "Pick that out of there and go git me a bag of sugar. Liddy Mae's gonna bake us a cake today."

"Pick it out of there yourself. He ain't workin' for you," Harrison said, getting up.

Carl pulled his gun and cocked it. "You just sit down, old man, and keep your nose out of this. Now, kid, I thank you'd better dig that four bits out of that spit can and git that sugar for Zeke. Otherwise I just may have to blow off a toe." He aimed the gun at Riley's boot.

"I . . . I'll git it," Riley stammered. He grimaced as he stuck his hand down into the full spittoon and fished up the coin. Then, shaking his hand to rid it of the spittle that clung to his fingers, he glared at Carl. "The store's closed 'til Mr. Edson gits out of church."

Zeke glanced at the big clock on the wall behind the bar. "Church will be done in ten minutes. Now you set us up with a bottle and four glasses, and then git your skinny ass down to the store and bring that sugar back here. You un'erstand me, boy?"

"I thank he oughta take it on out to the house and give it the Liddy Mae. That'll give us more time for drankin' and her more time for bakin'." Carl said.

Zeke rubbed his jaw. "Good idee. You take that sugar out to the house, boy, you un'erstand?"

Riley nodded and picked up four glasses from below the bar and set them down in front of the Hagans. Then he brought out a bottle of Harrison's cheapest whiskey and placed it next to the glasses. "I'll git that sugar now," he said.

He went out the rear door into the glaring sunlight

and headed for Edson's store. He grinned. He had stuck four fingers down inside those glasses from the same hand he had fished that half dollar out of the spittoon with. That'll teach them horses' asses not to mess with Thomas Jefferson Riley, he thought.

Mr. Edson had just opened the store when Riley entered. "The Hagan brothers sent me down fer a bag of sugar, Mr. Edson."

Edson scooped the sugar from a barrel and put it into a sack for Riley. "You be careful around those Hagans, Tom. They're not a very nice bunch."

"Yeah, I done found that out," Riley said. "Gimme one of them peppermint sticks too, Mr. Edson, and take it out of this." He put the fifty-cent piece on the counter.

Edson put a stick of the candy into the bag. "Do they know you're doing this with their money, Tom? They may not think it's right, you know."

"I don't give a hang what they thank," Riley said. "They made me fish that four bits out of a spittoon, so I got it comin'. Besides, I don't work for nothin'." He picked up the bag and left.

As Orville poured himself another shot of whiskey, he squinted and looked at Zeke's glass. "What's that brown crap a-slidin' down the side of your glass, Zeke?"

Zeke tilted the glass and stared open-mouthed. Then he looked at Harrison. "Hey, old man, don't you ever wash these thangs? This looks like . . . why that goddamned kid! He picked up these glasses with all that slobber from the spit can a-hangin' on his fangers. Wait 'til I git my hands on that scrawny little son of a—"

"It's your own damned fault," Harrison interrupted. "You forced him to stick his hand down into that filthy thing."

"Well, the least he coulda done was wash his hands," Orville commented.

"Now, that's the pot calling the kettle black," Harrison said, grinning. "What in the hell do you know about washing? You ain't been wet since you got caught in that rainstorm two years ago. And then you smelled like a wet dog for a month."

"You just shut up, old man, and give us some clean glasses," Bronco said, throwing the glass against the wall.

The ride out to the Hagan spread gave Riley plenty of time to think about meeting up with Liddy Mae again. He hadn't given her any more than a nod of recognition in the last eight years. It wasn't her looks that made him turn his head away. It was the constant ridiculing she had heaped on him over the years that did the trick. It had started on Valentine's Day at a church picnic down at the creek. He had laid out his undying love for her in a masterfully written poem in a Valentine's card he made by himself complete with a very cleverly drawn arrow right through the center of the big red heart. Her response, after she had stopped doubling up with laughter, was to show it to every girl she knew. Then, of course, she showed it to Elmer Washburn who made sure every boy had a chance to see it. From that day straight through to the last time he had seen her two months ago, she had made it a point to antagonize and embarrass him on a regular basis. So, the thought of being face to face with Liddy Mae once again was a tough bit of medicine to swallow. Well, he thought, at least it'll be an improvement over gittin' pushed around by them four piles of cow dung she calls brothers.

He dismounted and tied the reins to the hitching rail in front of the Hagan's house. He knocked on the door, but no one answered. He gave it a push and it swung open. He decided to leave the sugar on the kitchen table where Liddy Mae could find it. Then, retracing his steps, he started to leave.

A horse whinnied at the back of the house. Riley walked around to the rear and spotted it standing in front of the barn. He walked over to investigate. The barn door was open slightly so he stepped inside. Just as he was about to call her name, he heard voices coming from the hayloft. He walked over to the ladder and listened. Liddy Mae was on the verge of tears.

"It just ain't right, Elmer. You can't just walk away and leave me in the condition I'm in."

"I told you back when we first started, Liddy Mae, that something like this might happen, and you said not to worry about it. Well, I haven't, and now you're trying to hog-tie me. I told you I didn't want to be tied down."

"Well, what about me? I'm gonna be tied down the rest of my days. I'm too young for this." She began to cry.

Riley gulped. He hated to hear women cry and that included girls, even Liddy Mae. He knew he should stay out of their argument, but he liked Elmer Washburn even less than he did Liddy Mae, and this would be a chance to show him a thing or two about the proper way to treat a woman. He climbed the ladder.

Liddy Mae screamed and tried to cover her breasts with her blouse. Elmer stood and tucked in his shirt.

Riley couldn't believe his eyes. He had never seen a woman's bare breasts before. He never realized that they were so big.

"What in the hell are you doing sneaking around spying on people for, Riley? This ain't none of your damned business. I ought to punch you right in the nose," Elmer barked.

"You ought to learn how to treat women right is what you ought to do," Riley said.

Elmer swung a haymaker and caught Riley flush on

the nose. He dropped like a poled ox. Elmer stepped over Riley, climbed down the ladder, and took off running.

Liddy Mae screamed after him, "You're gonna be sorry you treated me thisaway, Elmer Washburn."

She then turned her attention to Riley. He was out but starting to show signs of recovery. A slow smile began to crinkle the corners of her mouth. He had been sweet on her at one time. It wouldn't take much to rekindle that spark. She dropped her blouse and raised Riley's head up and put her knee under his neck to make him more comfortable. She studied his face. He was no Elmer Washburn, but he would have to do.

Riley opened his eyes and stared up at Liddy Mae's bare, melon-heavy breasts suspended about five inches from his face. Things were blurred and he couldn't adjust his vision for a moment. He wondered why her eyes were so far apart. Then the nipples came into sharp focus. He started to sit up and they hit him smack in the face.

"You just take it easy now, Tommy. I'm gonna take care of you." She ran her fingers through his hair. Then suddenly she screamed.

Riley scrambled to his feet. Orville was standing on the loft ladder staring at them with his mouth ajar.

"Oh, my gawd!" Riley exclaimed.

"Why you mangy little . . . ," was all Orville managed to get out before Riley's boot hit him in the head and sent him flying backwards off the ladder.

Riley leaped off the loft to the floor below and flew through the door before Orville managed to yell for help. He rounded the front corner of the house just as the Hagan brothers came bounding through the rear door in response to Orville's calls. He was in the saddle and under way by the time they had reached the barn and heard Orville's story.

3

KENYON GAVE THE REINS A LIGHT TUG AND the line-back dun stopped and turned its head slightly. He dismounted and pulled the last of his food, two sticks of jerky and a biscuit, from his saddlebag. Untying the canteen, he walked over and sat beneath the overhanging branches of a Mexican blue oak that offered a thin patch of shade. The dun began to munch at small clumps of sacaton.

As Kenyon ate he thought about the trip he had just made to Hermosillo. His friend, Juan Eduardo Anderson had invited him to spend some time on his father's rancho. It had been a pleasant relief after the hard winter Kenyon had spent working for Juan's father, Sherman Anderson, in Oklahoma on his cattle ranch there. Anderson and the other cattlemen had suffered tremendous losses from the blizzard that paralyzed Kansas and Oklahoma.

Everyone had said the winter would go down as one of the most destructive on record. Kenyon had no doubts that it would. Ranchers for a 170-mile stretch had joined together to build a drift fence to keep the cattle from moving south when the cold weather came, but it didn't stop the longhorns. The first cattle to reach the fence had stood until they were trampled to death by others pressing forward. Eventually, a ramp of dead cattle had built up. Those in the rear marched over the carcasses and crossed to the other side of the fence, so they could continue their journey in search of warmer weather. When the blizzard had passed, thousands of cattle lay stacked in frozen heaps along the length of the drift line and across the land for hundreds of miles. Without cattle to tend, a cowboy had little luck finding work. Juan had worked right alongside Kenyon during the rough winter, and their friendship had grown strong, especially after Kenyon had pulled him from the icy river he had fallen into when his horse had broken through the crust.

Kenyon had enjoyed the month of rest, fiestas, and senoritas. Now it was time to get on with his life and find another job—somewhere.

He rose and tied the canteen behind the cantle. Then, mounting up, he headed the gelding down the *bajada* toward the valley below. The warm weather of spring had spread nature's palette of colors everywhere. Yellow cat's claw with its fragrant cylindrical spikes bloomed near dense stands of red-blossomed buckhorn cholla and flame-tipped ocotillo. White desert stars grew near the bases of screwbean mesquite with their large yellow tufts of stamens.

As the land became flatter, the vegetation gradually changed to a hardier type. The dun moved around a cluster of creosote and a pile of boulders. The outline of a wagon suddenly caught Kenyon's eye. Its square, sharp edges stood out in bold contrast against the soft-looking but spiny cholla cactus that covered the tongue and protruded through the weathered gray spokes of the front wheel. Part of the dead driver's skeleton was still visible, pinned to the back of the seat by the uneven shaft of an Apache arrow. Several vertebrae and the pelvic cross lay on the floor in front of the seat. The bones had been picked clean many years before, and the naked Arizona sun had bleached them white.

Kenyon wondered what kind of man the driver of the wagon had been. The frontier life was tough. It was tough for the men, very tough for their women, and it was hard on their animals and equipment.

A cloud of dust in the distance drew Kenyon's attention. The line-back dun, feeling the forward shift of Kenyon's weight, started to move, but a tug on the reins stopped him as the big man stood in the stirrups. He could make out a single rider, his pinto at a dead run, heading toward a low saddle in the distance. In another moment four riders about a hundred yards behind the pinto broke into view. It was obvious that the four riders were rapidly closing the distance between themselves and the lone rider. Nobody rode like that unless there was trouble brewing, and the odds of four against one were not to Kenyon's liking. Of course, it could be a posse, and if that were the case, he wouldn't interfere.

He shifted his weight again, and the dun, attuned to his slightest movement, headed through the mesquite at a quick pace. He turned the line-back in a direction that would shorten the distance between himself and the riders and nudged it in the flank. It moved down an arroyo that cut through the scarred face of the valley floor and offered Kenyon some protection from the rider's view.

They had evidently caught up with the pinto they were chasing. The sounds coming from up ahead indicated that they had stopped. Kenyon didn't like the laughter and hooting that filtered through the creosote bushes that fringed the arroyo. It wasn't the good-natured kind a man might find among friends. It had a meaner ring to it, the kind a bully uses to frighten whomever he intends to beat on.

The arroyo's sandy bottom had begun to change to a heavy mixture of rock and gravel. Kenyon couldn't go any further on the gelding without alerting the men up ahead, so he dismounted. He put his hand on the dun's nose as a signal to be quite; then, drawing his

Colt .45 from its holster, he climbed quietly out of the arroyo.

The riders were obviously enjoying whatever they were doing to the man they had caught. Kenyon could tell from the noise they were making. He could see patches of color from their clothing through the *palo verde* and mesquite, but he couldn't get a clear view. There was an outcrop of rock to the left of where they were grouped. If he could move around the clumps of jumping cholla, he felt certain the rock would give him the protection he wanted and provide the element of surprise he needed.

"Carl, you and Orville give Bronco a hand and strip off them pants and boots."

Kenyon didn't like the sound of the voice or the order it had given. He quickened his pace and reached the rock undetected. Then he got his first real look at the strangers. The one on the ground immediately got his attention. He was a skinny kid not more than seventeen. He studied the faces of the three men holding the kid down.

Kenyon recognized the one pinning the boy's arms to the ground as a man he had seen on a New Mexico cattle drive two years before, an ill-tempered hard case named Bronco Hagan. He was nothing but trouble, as Kenyon recalled. The other three weren't exactly what he would judge to be ideal company. There seemed to be a strong ugly family resemblance between them. No doubt they're brothers, Kenyon thought.

He turned his attention to Zeke Hagan, the biggest and meanest of the group. Zeke stood gloating over the prostrate form of Thomas Jefferson Riley now lying spread-eagled and nude except for a shirt.

Pulling a knife from a scabbard in his boot, Zeke leaned over Riley and tossed it back and forth between his hands just above Riley's groin. When the boy's jaw went slack with fear, Zeke straightened up smiling.

"Well now, Mr. Riley, what have you got to say for yourself?"

Riley kicked and tried to squirm loose.

"What's the matter, kid," Zeke continued, "the cat got your tongue? Well, he's gonna have a pair of balls to go with it in just about one minute. Ain't that right, boys?"

He laughed while the others joined him with catcalls and hoots.

"What do you want to cut on me fer?" Riley asked, his voice breaking with fear.

"Why?" Zeke's eyes narrowed. "You hear that, boys? This skinny-ass little yearlin' wants to know why." Then, swishing the long blade back and forth menacingly, he let his smile return gradually, but there was no humor in it. "Cause you dishonored our baby sister, you mangy little bastard. She's gonna have a baby now 'cause of you. Liddy Mae ain't nothin' but a baby herself. She ain't but sixteen years old." Zeke clinched his teeth together and forced out the words. "You know that . . . huh?" He kicked Riley in the leg.

"I didn't do nothin' to your sister 'cept to look at her," Riley complained.

Bronco grabbed Riley under the chin with one hand. "Then how come her belly's swellin' up? How come she's in a family way?"

"Yeah," Carl said, butting in. "A girl don't git no swelled up belly from just lookin'. Does she, Orville?"

Orville shrugged, not quite sure of what his answer should be.

"It couldn't have been me," Riley said. "I ain't done nothin' to her but look, and I only done that once . . . just before Orville climbed into the hayloft. It must have been Elmer Washburn," he said hastily. "She's pretty sweet on him, you know."

Zeke kicked Riley again in the hip. "Liar! It was you that done it." Then he smiled coldly. "I'm gonna make you into a gelding, boy. Then you ain't never gonna mount no girl again."

Zeke swished the knife back and forth while leaning over Riley's prostrate form.

"Hold it!" Kenyon's voice echoed off the walls of the draw making it seem louder than it was.

Zeke straightened up and spun around. He flipped the knife to his left hand and started to reach for his gun but found that he was staring down the barrel of Kenyon's Colt and decided against it.

"Drop the knife and move away from the boy," Kenyon continued, his voice calm. "You're not cuttin' on anybody."

Zeke stepped away from Riley but held the knife while he answered. "This just ain't none of your business, stranger. My advice to you is keep your nose where it belongs."

Kenyon grinned. "I don't give a damn for your advice, fella. I told you to drop that Arkansas toothpick and here you are still hangin' on to it." He fired one shot. It struck the blade of Zeke's knife and sent it spinning to the ground. It also set Zeke to doing a fast fandango while he tried to stop his hand from stinging.

Kenyon swung the muzzle toward the other three Hagans. "Let him up and hand him his pants."

Carl moved with considerable vigor, but Orville and Bronco were slow and surly.

"Unbuckle your gun belts and let 'em drop on the ground." The men complied. "Now take off your boots," Kenyon ordered.

"My boots?" Orville asked, as Carl sat down and removed his.

"Your boots," Kenyon answered.

"I ain't walking back home barefoot for you or nobody else," Orville growled.

Kenyon fired another shot neatly ripping the heel from one of Orville's boots and sending him falling on top of Carl.

"Now what in the hell did you have to go and do that for?" Orville complained. "Them's twenty-dollar boots!"

"They're only worth ten now," Kenyon answered.

Riley scrambled into his clothes and turned to face Kenyon. "I don't know who you are, Mister, but I'm sure beholding to you. I want you to know that I ain't done nothin' I'm ashamed of. That's what I tried to tell these Hagans here, but they just wouldn't listen."

"Yeah, they look thicker than a fence post," Kenyon observed. "You get on your horse now and bring mine from beyond those rocks, then scare the other ones away."

Riley did as he was told.

Kenyon once again addressed the Hagans. "I'll drop these boots and guns a couple of miles back down this draw."

Zeke snarled, "I don't know who you are, stranger, but I'll tell you this. You ain't seen the last of the Hagans."

"Wait a minute," Bronco said. "Don't I know you? Yeah . . . I think I do." Turning to Zeke he continued. " 'Member when I worked that cattle drive in New Mexico a couple of years back? This dude was one of the drovers. Ain't that right?" he asked turning again toward Kenyon.

"Yeah," Kenyon said smiling, "I couldn't forget a face like yours."

"I didn't like you then, and I sure as hell don't like you now," Bronco said. "You're just settin' yourself up to be blowed in two next time we meet."

"You really know how to strike fear in a man," Kenyon said grinning.

"And don't you think you're gettin' off scot-free

neither, Riley," Zeke called. "Just 'cause this stranger here saved them wavos of yourn this time don't mean I ain't gonna catch up with you one of these days. And when I do, boy, you'll be fit to sing with the ladies' choir."

"Let's go, kid," Kenyon said. He headed down the draw with the Hagans' gun belts looped around the saddle horn and four pairs of boots tucked under his arm.

Riley followed behind, admiring Kenyon's broad shoulders. Then wearing a big grin, he rode up beside him, "Guess I ought to introduce myself. I'm Thomas Jefferson Riley. I must look like a real horse's tail to you . . . I mean . . . lettin' four louts like them Hagan brothers catch me and make me shuck my britches."

Kenyon chuckled. "The Horse-tail Kid. Well, I wouldn't let gettin' caught worry me none, Kid. Four against one is pretty high odds. I don't think many men could have done much better."

Riley grinned again. "You really thank so?" They rode in silence for a ways while Riley digested the compliment. "Where are you headin'?" he asked after a bit. "I ain't tryin' to be nosy, I want you to know. It's just that, well, I know I can't stay around here now with those four Hagans after me, so I was wonderin' if I could, you know, kinda tag along with you for awhile?"

"It's a free country," Kenyon answered with a smile.

"Where you from?" Riley asked.

"Wherever I hang my hat."

Riley studied Kenyon's rugged, handsome face. This feller sure ain't much for talkin', he thought. He knew it wasn't right to pry into the man's life, but heckfire, this stranger had saved him from becoming the only boy soprano west of the Mississippi and, well, he liked the way the stranger looked and moved and used a gun. Riley liked everything about him, and that meant he had to get to know the man a little better.

"You got any kinfolk in these parts?" he asked.

"Nope."

Riley scratched his head. He would have to be a little slier in his approach. "Where are you headin'?"

"Tuscon," Kenyon replied. "I go wherever I can find work."

"Well," Riley said, eager to add to the conversation. "It's mighty good you're planning on going on to Tucson and not stay around in these parts. I've lived here all my life, and there ain't no work around this place; I'll tell you that." Riley glanced at his companion to get his reaction. There was none, so he continued. "I've been alone since my ma died last summer. Been doin' sort of odd jobs to keep goin'. I damned near starved to death this winter, so I'm more than ready to move on, Mr. . . . ah . . ."

"Just call be Kenyon. Folks never took to my given name, and I can't abide by it either."

"I want to thank you again, Mr. Kenyon," Riley said, "for savin' my hide."

"Your what?" Kenyon asked, smiling.

"Well, at least two round patches of it," Riley answered and they both laughed.

Riley liked Kenyon's easy laugh. It had a nice low pitch like his speaking voice. It was the kind he would like to have himself. His own laugh tended to rise high enough to punch holes in the clouds, and it made everybody gawk and laugh at him when he got tickled.

Kenyon stopped and threw the Hagan brother's boots and holsters down by the side of the trail. Then he took his Colt and broke the firing pin off each of their guns and dropped them next to the boots.

"I reckon this is far enough for a bunch of tenderfeet to walk, don't you?"

Riley dismounted. "Yeah," he replied, "but I thank

we ought to add a little surprise to their boots—just as a reward for their kindness to others." He took a knife from his pocket and cut some small tips from a cholla cactus. Then, dropping one tip down inside each boot, he shook them so that the cactus balls would settle to the front. After stepping on the toe of each boot to make sure that the cactus spines were firmly embedded in the leather, he mounted up again.

"That ought to make them bastards hop," he said.

"You're downright vicious, Kid."

Riley grinned. "Ain't it the truth."

"Tell me about this Hagan girl," Kenyon said, looking over at Riley as he spoke.

Riley felt his face getting hot. He looked down hoping that Kenyon hadn't noticed. He had no intention of letting Kenyon know he'd been fool enough to get involved in an argument between Liddy Mae and Elmer or that Elmer had gotten the better of him in a fight. Why had he tried to defend Liddy Mae in the first place? This whole thing had been her fault, her and them big tits she had flopped in his face. Since he didn't have any firsthand experience, he decided to tell Kenyon what the other boys had said about her.

"Well, she ain't too bad a looker," Riley began, "but she's too loose, if you know what I mean."

Kenyon raised an eyebrow. "I think I get it, yeah."

"I didn't really do nothin' with her myself," Riley continued.

Kenyon eyed him curiously. "Why not?"

Riley gulped. Somehow this conversation wasn't going too well. "Ah . . . I . . . ah . . . just didn't have enough time, I guess," Riley muttered.

"Enough time? How long have you known her?"

"It ain't that. I mean, I've known her all my life. It's just that . . . well, I reckon I'm kind of shy." He shrugged.

"But not too shy to look," Kenyon said grinning.

Feeling the need to pump himself up a bit in front of Kenyon, Riley added, "The lookin' was beginnin' to get interestin' though when that dumb brother of hers broke in on us. I was just barely able to git out of there and grab my horse. They lit out on my tail and caught me back yonder. They'd have gelded me too if you hadn't come along."

"That's pretty strong punishment for just lookin'," Kenyon said dryly.

"Well, that's all I done," Riley answered, "and you can bet me that's the last time I'm ever gonna mess around with some dumb girl."

"Just lookin' ain't exactly what I call messin' around," Kenyon said, "but I guess it's a start."

They rode on in silence until they reached the edge of town, six dusty buildings spread out down a badly rutted road.

Riley began to shift nervously in his saddle. "How long do you figure it'll take them Hagans to make it back into town?"

Kenyon smiled as Riley peered over his shoulder. "Well, I figure it'll take 'em an hour or so to walk barefoot down to where we dropped their guns. Then, it'll take 'em half the day to pick all those cactus needles you so kindly presented them with, out of the toes of their boots . . ."

"What if they git them horses right away?" Riley interrupted.

"After that," Kenyon continued unphased, "they'll probably have to walk over hell's half acre and half of Georgia to round up their horses."

"What if they just have to whistle to git them horses to come a-runnin'? Then they'll strap on them guns and come a-lookin' fer us."

"You're kind of full of *what if's* ain't you, Kid. When they finally make it into town, which I'm inclined to believe won't occur 'til tomorrow mornin' at the earliest, they'll have to have a gunsmith repair the damage I did to their hand guns. Of course, they could get hold of some rifles somewhere, but I'd say we've got enough time to have a sit-down supper without rushin' through the dessert."

Riley's face fell. He wanted them to rush out of town. Forget the dessert! "Oh . . . well I'll just git some things from my room, and then I'll be ready to go right away," Riley said. "Where are you goin' to be, so I can meet you?"

"I'm going to have a drink at the local saloon and then grab something to eat," Kenyon answered.

"Harrison's here is the only place in town for drinkin'. They got some good lookin' women workin' in there too," he added.

"For a kid who's just sworn off females, you sure seem to know what's goin' on."

Riley grinned. "Ain't nothin' wrong with just admirin'—from a distance, that is. See you in a few minutes."

"Here," Kenyon said taking a couple of dollars from his pocket. "Pick us up some food for the trail. I'll leave my horse tied up here in front of the saloon. If you get back before I'm finished eatin', put the stuff into these saddle bags. You know what to get, don't you? Hardtack, jerky, coffee . . ."

"Why, heck yeah," Riley said. "I've done this kind of stuff lots of times before." He turned the pinto and rode down the street.

"Right," Kenyon said, shaking his head.

The wisdom of taking the Horse-tail Kid along began to gnaw away at him. Kenyon had always traveled alone and liked it, but there were times when the loneliness of the trail could drive a man crazy. Maybe the kid wouldn't be bad company after all. If he didn't like the arrangement, he and the kid could always ride different trails.

Kenyon looked at the front of Harrison's Saloon. It had the same weathered clapboard siding and the same faded lettering as most other cow-town bars he'd been in. Only those businesses that prospered from the trail drives ever bothered with a fresh coat of paint, and that wasn't too often. A pall of stale cigarette smoke mingled with the odor of cheap bar whiskey and hung like a veil behind the bat-wing doors.

Harrison stopped polishing the pitted mahogany bar as the doors creaked. He quickly glanced over at the two barmaids who stood talking to a customer and noisily cleared his throat. When one of them, Sally, looked up, he gave his head a quick nod toward Kenyon; then, he turned and smiled.

"Howdy, stranger. What'll it be?"

"A glass of beer."

Harrison drew the beer from the tap and set the glass down in front of Kenyon. "Just passing through?"

"More or less."

Sally moved down the bar toward Kenyon. Well, she sighed, any cowpoke who looks as good as this one is sure a lot better than the usual that comes in here. Most of 'em ain't worth spit. This might be a good Sunday yet, she thought.

Kenyon studied her as she approached. She had seen a hard life and showed it. Heavy makeup failed to conceal the deep lines that a thousand disappointments had etched into her face. The corners of her mouth turned down, blending into two unbroken lines that ended somewhere beneath her chin, and gave it the separated look that Kenyon had seen once on a ventriloquist's wooden dummy. The vacant look in her eyes changed as she flashed a smile.

"Howdy, cowboy." Her voice was deep with rough edges. It might have been able to quicken a man's pulse some twenty winters ago, but endless glasses of cheap liquor had replaced a once-soft huskiness with a quality akin to gravel crushed beneath the iron-bound wheel of a freight wagon. "I ain't seen you before," she went on. "You new in town?"

Kenyon smiled back. "Just passin' through. Any other time I'd be pleased to buy you a drink ma'am, but I'm a little down on my luck."

Sally's smile disappeared momentarily and then returned, but this time there was genuine warmth behind it.

"A pity," she replied, looking Kenyon over from boots to hat. "It would have been interesting."

"Is there a place to eat around here?" Kenyon asked as she turned to leave.

"There's a Mex'can place at the end of the road. A gal named Rosita runs it. She's fatter than a Poland China 'cause she can't stay away from her own cookin' and boy is it good."

Kenyon touched the brim of his hat. "Much obliged." He finished his beer and stood. "If a young kid named Riley comes in here lookin' for me, tell him I'll be back in about half an hour. Will you?"

Sally laughed and turned to Harrison. "Ain't Riley that gangling kid that sweeps out the place for you on Sunday mornings?"

Harrison grinned. "The one and only."

She turned once again to Kenyon. "That kid's gun-shy when it comes to women. He ain't never been closer to me than half the length of this bar. But if he comes in, I'll shout at him and tell him to wait." She laughed again. "That is if he don't bolt and run when I start talkin'." She moved away, still laughing as Kenyon went through the swinging doors.

"Hello, Tom," Mr. Edson said as Riley walked in. "Did the Hagans say anything about that stick candy?"

"Them Hagans tried to make a gelding out of me

today, Mr. Edson. Luckily a good friend of mine stopped 'em in time."

"Maybe they were just kidding around. Surely they wouldn't do a thing like that to a person."

"They were dead earnest, Mr. Edson, so I'm leavin' with my friend as soon as I get some things from my room and buy a few supplies for the trail. I'm sorry I won't be able to sweep out the store for you no more."

"Do you have any money, Tom? Where will you go? How will you live?"

He shrugged. "I don't rightly know, but if my friend can do it, I sure can too. We'll go wherever we can find work, and home will be wherever we hang our hats."

"Here, Tom. It isn't much," Edson said, taking some money from his change drawer, "but it might help tide you over until you can get some work. You've certainly earned it."

Riley looked down and scuffed the toe of his boot on the floor. "You didn't have to go and do this, Mr. Edson. I'll git by alright."

"I have no doubt that you will, Tom, but this will help out. Now, you go get your things, and I'll fill up a sack for you."

Riley grinned as he headed back to his room.

Kenyon entered the La Paloma, a squat adobe building that doubled as a cafe and living quarters for Rosita Herrera and her dark-eyed, black-haired children.

He ordered a stack of hot corn tortillas and a plate of steaming frijoles; then, he settled back to study the construction of Rosita's cafe while she prepared his supper.

He had been away from this part of the Southwest for several years, and one of the things he'd missed were the adobe buildings. They were put together from the land itself, and they were part of it. The adobe clay and straw were formed into thick heavy bricks. Some of them still carried the handprints of a worker or the naked track of a lizard or dog who'd passed that way before the bricks had fully relinquished their moisture. In summer the adobe's two-foot-thick walls could temper the sun by more than twenty degrees, making an adobe an inviting oasis in a sky-scorched land of heat and dust. In winter the walls' protection kept the interior warm and comforting.

The restaurant's ceiling was made from the ribs of the giant saguaro. Bound tightly together and lashed with rawhide strips to a lodgepole pine that served as a beam, they formed an almost impenetrable web that supported the roof.

Rosita arrived with the food and drew Kenyon's attention back to a more immediate need.

One of Rosita's small daughters arrived with a bowl of hot sauce.

"Usted quiere salsa, señor?"

"Es picante?" Kenyon asked.

The little girl smiled. "Sí, señor, es muy picante."

"Bueno," Kenyon replied. "I like it hot!"

He spread several large spoonfuls over his plate of beans and began eating.

The little girl stood to one side watching and waiting.

After the second bite, Kenyon could have sworn he was eating molten iron.

It was obvious to Rosita's daughter that Kenyon was finding the sauce much hotter than he had anticipated, for he began looking around for some cooling liquid to drink.

"Cerveza, señor?" she asked.

Kenyon laughed. "Sí, sí, dos cervezas, pronto!"

The girl scampered away and quickly returned with two beers.

Kenyon muttered a "gracias" and drank one without stopping.

After his breathing had returned to normal, he watched the little girl clean up a nearby table. That little beauty's gonna be a heartbreaker some day, he thought, as he got up and paid his bill.

Kenyon saw Riley's pinto next to his gelding as he crossed the road. When a rider stopped next to the pinto and tied his horse to the rail, Kenyon noticed the pinto shy to one side with an unusual movement. He inspected the pinto's hooves and found one without a shoe.

Upon entering Harrison's saloon, Kenyon noticed that the customers were gathered around the card table at the far end of the room. He looked at Harrison. "What's goin' on, a hot game?"

"No, it just started."

"Is Riley here?"

"Yeah, he's gamblin' the wages I just paid him."

Kenyon walked back to the table. "Riley, your pinto needs a new shoe. You want me to have one put on for you?"

"Well, I ought to take care of that myself."

"That's okay, I'll do it. It's bad luck to take a man away from a card game after he's just sat down. I'll be back in half an hour or so."

"I'll be right here a-playin'."

Kenyon sized up the other three players, a drover and two mean-looking miners.

"Don't lose it all, Kid. You'll need some for the trail."

Riley grinned. "I ain't plannin' on losin'."

Kenyon left to find the blacksmith.

Just after he had paid the blacksmith and was starting to lead the pinto out to the road, Sally walked up.

"Harrison said to tell you, you'd better get back in

a hurry. Riley's winnin' but them two rattlesnakes he's takin' most of the money from ain't gonna stand losin' much longer.''

"Thanks, ma'am, I appreciate your tellin' me."

"You go on. I'll take your horse back to the hitchin' rail."

"Much obliged." He touched the brim of his hat in a thank-you gesture then took off at a fast pace.

As he entered the saloon and walked back to the table, he could tell that the loser was getting angry from the pitch of his voice.

"I'll call you," Riley said, throwing several silver dollars into the center of the table.

"Aces and queens," the loser said, reaching for the pot.

"Wait a minute," Riley countered. "I got three deuces."

Kenyon watched the loser deftly palm a card from the discard pile while he distracted Riley's attention with his other hand.

"Let me see those cards," the loser growled.

Riley set three deuces, a ten, and a four down on the table. The loser picked them up adding the one he'd palmed earlier. Throwing them down on the table one by one he counted them out.

"How about this king of spades here kid? You played with six cards. This is five-card draw. That ain't exactly what I call honest playin'. Looks like I win, don't it?"

"Hey, wait a minute," the drover said. "That's one of the cards . . ." His voice trailed off as the loser gave him a mean glare.

"What was that?" the loser demanded.

"Noth . . . nothing," the drover stammered. "Guess I was wrong."

"I don't know where you got that card, mister, but

it sure wasn't from my hand," Riley said. "I won this pot fair and square."

"You callin' me a liar, boy?" the loser said rising. "Ask anybody here. They saw me count out them cards. There was six of them."

"That's true," Kenyon said. "There were six cards, Kid."

The loser grinnned.

"The five you put down and the one he palmed from the discard pile," Kenyon added.

The loser reached for his gun.

Kenyon's hand was a blur of speed. When it stopped moving, it held a big Colt .45 and it was pointed at the loser's chest. He smiled. "A card game ain't nothin' to get killed over."

From the corner of his eye, Kenyon saw the loser's friend move. Swinging the Colt in a fast arc to the right, he brought the barrel alongside the miner's jaw, dropping him like a sack of beans. Keeping his eyes on the loser, he swung the .45 toward him once again. "I guess his friend lost interest in the game, Kid," he said to Riley who sat staring openmouthed. "Pick up your money and move out."

As Riley stepped through the door, Kenyon backed out and grinned at Harrison. "If you keep that sorehead away from his gun 'til we mount up, I won't have to shoot him."

Riley stuck his head back inside. "So long, Mr. Harrison."

"Goodbye, Riley, and good luck."

Kenyon and the Kid were almost out of town when the loser emerged and fired a parting shot. It thudded harmlessly into a clump of ocotillo.

After they'd ridden a mile or so, Kenyon eased up and brought the dun down to a slow trot to let him breathe.

"Shouldn't we keep ridin'?" Riley asked.

Kenyon grinned. "No point runnin' the horses. Nobody's apt to follow us."

"But that guy was awful mad," Riley observed.

"When a man knows he's been had in a draw," Kenyon said, "he ain't about to press his luck a second time. And his pardner won't be awake for another hour."

"I'm sure beholdin' to you," Riley said, "for the second time in the same day too. Seems like you've done nothin' but get me out of trouble ever since we met."

"Sometimes trouble comes and there ain't nothin' a man can do to avoid it," Kenyon said. "Other times, a man should know when to walk away and let things be."

"Did I do somethin' wrong?" Riley asked.

"You've got to watch people a little closer, Kid. Sometimes they let you in on what's goin' to happen long before they realize it themselves. You can learn a lot by watchin' a man's eyes. That loser's eyes were burnin' holes right through you."

"What do you think I should have done?" Riley asked.

"First thing, I reckon, is don't play cards with a sorehead. Watch the players at the table for a couple of hands. The ones that can't stand losin' are easy to spot. Once you put your cards down, don't let anybody pick them up the way he did. Make him count the cards lyin' on the table. It's harder to slip in a palmed card that way. Other than that, I'd say carry a gun and learn how to use it. That way you don't have to back down when you know you're right . . . unless you're outnumbered or the other guy's a gunslinger . . ."

"Will you teach me, Mr. Kenyon?"

"Teach you what? And don't call me 'mister.'"

"Teach me to shoot? I won enough money in that card game to buy myself a real nice gun. Will you?"

"Yeah . . . I guess so," Kenyon answered reluctantly.

"Where did you learn to shoot?" Riley asked.

"Who said I could?" Kenyon replied.

Riley looked startled for a moment. Then he grinned. "The way you drew. Ain't no beginner can draw like that. I'll bet you can shoot the eye out of a rattlesnake at thirty paces."

"I couldn't hit a bull in the ass with a barn door," Kenyon answered.

Riley's grin broke into a chuckle. "Yeah, sure . . ."

Kenyon grinned. "Ok, Kid. When we get to Tucson we'll get you a decent gun and a couple of wagon loads of bullets, and I'll show you how to squeeze the trigger."

"Yahoo!" Riley yelled, and they laughed together. After they'd ridden for a ways, Riley brought up the subject again. "All kiddin' aside, Mr. Kenyon, I mean . . . Kenyon, where did you learn how to handle a gun and shoot like you do? You sure blew that knife out of Zeke Hagan's hand clean enough."

"I just picked it up here and there. Didn't you ever have a gun of your own?"

"Yeah, I had me a rifle for killin' varmints, but my ma said farmers don't have no need for handguns."

"How did your pa feel?"

"He ran off to Alaska when I was ten. Told my ma he'd send for us. We never heard nothin' from him after that. Don't know whether he'd still alive or what. I don't much care neither. I can take care of myself."

Kenyon glanced at Riley. "You're right, Kid. I could tell that right off first time I saw you." There was a hint of humor in his voice.

Riley studied Kenyon's expression trying to decide whether or not he was being kidded. Then he mumbled, "Well, most of the time, anyway."

Kenyon burst out laughing and Riley joined in enjoying the joke on himself.

The next several days went by quicker than Kenyon had ever remembered any days passing before. Most of the time was spent either laughing at or with the Kid.

4

KENYON STUDIED THE AREA BEFORE HIM FOR a campsite. The desert's flowered floor hid deep-furrowed ridges, evidence of the cutting power of the first rains of spring. The water had sculpted the sand and softened its hard features with an explosion of color. Every hue of nature's variety grew in profusion. A small stream of water still worked at the banks of a nearly dry stream bed.

Kenyon considered it a miracle that there was still a trickle of water in the stream. The rain had fallen almost two weeks before, and the days following had been hot and dry the way today had started out. Then around noon it had clouded up, and now there was a possibility that it might rain again. He knew it would not be wise to camp near the creek itself. He had known men who had drowned from a rain that fell in the mountains ten miles away, and by the time the runoff had reached the desert, the dry stream bed where they had camped had become a raging torrent of water five feet deep.

He chose as their campsite for the night a small mesa with a cluster of boulders at one end. Those big rocks would help keep the wind that often sprang up in the early morning hours off their backs, and there was an ample supply of saguaro ribs nearby to use for fuel, so he dismounted.

"Why don't you rustle up some wood, and I'll break

out the coffee pot," Kenyon said as he loosened the girth around the dun's belly.

Riley soon returned with half a dozen saguaro ribs and an armload of dry brush.

"Look at this, Kenyon. What the devil you think this is?" Riley said, holding up what he'd found. "It looks like a big old moccasin or something."

"You hit it right on the mark," Kenyon said. "They call them Apache boots."

"Sure they do," Riley answered, chuckling.

"That's what they're called. It's a nest made by a woodpecker inside the saguaro cactus," Kenyon explained.

"Well, I'll be jiggered," Riley said.

Riley soon had a hot fire going, and Kenyon's coffee pot perked away, sending out an invisible cloud of delicious aroma.

"There's only one thing that smells better than fresh coffee perkin' on a camp fire," Riley observed, "and that's bacon."

"That's right," Kenyon said. "Just remember that if you have to go through Indian country. Those are two things you don't cook out in the open. You can smell 'em a mile away and an Apache can double that."

"I never thought of that," Riley answered seriously. "That's good to know. You ever fight any Indians?"

"I had a set to with some Chiricahuas once near the Mexican border. They were tryin' to make off with our horses."

"Did you kill any of them?" Riley asked with unbridled enthusiasm.

Kenyon studied Riley before answering.

"The only time I've ever had to kill a man was in self-defense. They weren't out to kill me, just steal the horses. It's part of their way of life. They don't look upon stealing horses as a bad thing to do. It shows their bravery, provides them with food, and gives them the means to buy wives for themselves. It's a natural thing to do from their point of view. Of course, if it's your horse, you're not likely to agree with them."

"They eat horses?"

Kenyon grinned. "They prefer horses and mules to deer and elk."

"Did they hit you with a tomahawk or anything?"

"Yeah," Kenyon said, "one of 'em hit me right alongside the head with a cow chip. Damned near knocked me out of the saddle too."

"Now you're joshin' me," Riley said.

"Listen, Kid, when you're fightin' Apaches you've got to expect the unexpected."

The evening chill came down like a giant cloak lowered over the desert floor with the delicate touch of a new young bride. It started at the top of Kenyon's shoulders and gradually spread down the back chilling him so slowly and gently that he was completely unaware of being cold until he got up from the fire's edge and suddenly gave himself a giant shake. Then it seemed to penetrate his bones.

"It's colder than a gambler's heart, Riley. I think we'd better bank up that fire pretty good tonight, or we'll both be corpses in the mornin'."

Riley shook himself and agreed. After he'd built up the fire, he spread his horse blanket down and curled up on top of it.

Kenyon dug a small pit and filled it with hot coals. Then, placing a covering of sand several inches deep over the coals, he made his bed on top.

As the first light of the dawn tinged the lower edges of the eastern sky, Riley stirred in his blankets. Then, suddenly, both eyes popped wide open.

He could feel the weight of something on his blanket that wasn't there the night before. The rattler, seeking warmth, had coiled up near Riley's knees. Riley let out a shriek that would have stirred Abe Lincoln in his grave, and at the same time threw his bedding blanket, rattler and all, into the air.

Kenyon sat bolt upright to find an angry rattlesnake landing on him. He rolled to one side drawing his gun from its holster in one smooth motion. Fortunately the rattler, being cold-blooded, had not yet reached his operating temperature and was sluggish in his movements. Kenyon sent a .45 slug through the snake's neck neatly severing its head from the five-foot-long body.

"I don't mind sharin' a man's bedmate if it's the right kind, Riley, but that sure as hell doesn't include snakes."

"I'm . . . sorry," Riley mumbled. "I didn't mean to throw him on top on you. He just scared the hell out of me."

"Well, he sure didn't do much for me, I'll tell you," Kenyon mumbled. "Come on. Let's have some coffee and we'll head for Tucson."

The coals were blown into life and a pot of coffee was soon sending out its magnetic aroma, which drew the two cowboys to the fire's edge.

"How far you figure it is to town?" Riley asked.

Kenyon gripped the metal handle of the pot with a large blue bandana and poured two cups of the steaming brew. "We ought to be there by early afternoon."

"Is it a nice town?"

"I don't know what you mean by *nice*, but it's got everything a man needs to keep body and soul together—liquor, women, food, and a place to sleep."

"I ain't never seen Tucson before," Riley said.

"If we can't get work right away, I don't reckon you'll see much of it this time either," Kenyon replied. "That is, if you still want to tag along with me."

"I sure do," Riley commented. "If we can't find work, are we gonna move on?"

"It's either that or put on a tin bill and scratch manure with the chickens," Kenyon answered.

Riley was still chuckling about that as they put out the fire and headed for town.

Tucson had more hustle and activity than any place Riley had ever seen.

Everywhere he looked there was something going on. A dozen men standing atop huge freight wagons were unloading their goods on the edge of the boardwalk in front of several stores. The blacksmith shop had two men working full time. Riley was amazed at the number of people strolling up and down the streets.

Kenyon stopped in front of a saloon. He pulled some money from his pocket and handed it to Riley. "Why don't you go to that store up the street and get us some more jerky. From the way you put that stuff away, you'd better buy half a steer. If there ain't no work around here, we're gonna have to head for Phoenix, and we'll be needing some meat. I'll ask around inside and see if anyone needs a couple of good hands."

Riley beamed at the idea of being considered a "good hand." He took the money, eased his little pinto around Kenyon's dun, and headed for the store.

Kenyon slapped his hat against the side of his leg to remove the trail dust as he edged up to the bar. Then, taking the big bandana from his pocket, he wiped the sweatband on the inside of his Stetson and placed it on the bar. "A beer," he said to the frail balding bartender.

"From the looks of that dust, I'd say you've rode a fur piece," the bartender said, as he set the glass full of the brew down on the bar's discolored surface.

"Yeah, it's been a long one," Kenyon said. "Know of anyone that needs a couple of good hands around here?"

"I think Nahan's General Store is lookin' for somebody."

"I ain't no storekeeper," Kenyon replied taking a sip. "I mean punchin' cows or wranglin' horses."

"Well, not that I've heard tell of," the bartender said. "Course I don't hear about ever' job that comes along, mind you. It seems to me, though, that cowhands bein' the natural born drifters that they are, they move along after they've worked a month or two and gotten drunk a couple of times, so there must be *some* ranches around here that need a few drovers. You might talk to old A. J. Spalding. He's an agent for a cattle-buyin' comp'ny, and he'd prob'ly know if they was an openin' somewheres."

"Where do I find old A.J.?" Kenyon asked.

"His office is just past the general store up the street."

"Much obliged," Kenyon said finishing his beer. He put on his hat and surveyed the saloon. "How can you stand workin' inside all the time and especially in a dismal place like this?"

The man looked up; a large grin creased his face. "It ain't much, but it beat the hell out of lookin' at nothin' but the south end of a northbound herd and breathin' trail dust and stale farts in a bunkhouse."

Kenyon chuckled. "I guess you got me there." He stepped through the swinging doors and into the sun-drenched afternoon. Up the street he could see a small crowd of people milling around watching five men on horseback ride out of town. Kenyon thought he saw a little pinto in the center of the group of horses just as they turned the corner, but he wasn't sure. He decided to go up and see what the excitement was about.

When he reached the crowd, some of the townspeople were still talking about the incident that had just happened.

"That kid sure looked scared. I wonder what he done to them jaspers?"

"I don't know, but he's gonna be awful sorry when

they get through with him. That was the meanest lookin' group I've seen in a long time."

Kenyon spoke to the man who'd just finished talking. "Was the kid you spoke of about seventeen? Kinda tall and gawky and ridin' a pinto?"

"That's him alright, mister. He a friend of yours?"

Kenyon didn't answer but took off in a run back to the saloon's hitching post for his horse. Once mounted on the dun's back, he kicked the big gelding into a gallop and headed in the direction the Hagans had taken Riley. After he reached the edge of town, he nudged the line-back into a dead run. Within minutes he crested a ridge and could see the group of horses up ahead. He reined the dun to a halt and waited near some rocks so as not to make a silhouette. Then, after the group turned a bend in the road, he took off at a gallop to catch up. When he reached the bend, he could see the last of the Hagan brothers disappearing into a cluster of big rocks to the left of the road. Approaching with caution, he slowed the dun to a walk and stopped by the rocks. Dismounting, he moved quickly between the big boulders until he could hear muffled voices ahead.

Zeke Hagan was speaking. "Orville, you git back yonder to the road and make sure nobody comes ridin' up on us like last time."

"How come I don't get to watch?" Orville grumbled.

"This ain't no damned medicine show," Zeke barked. "You want to see what this boy's agates look like when I git through cuttin' 'em off, I'll leave 'em on this here rock for you. Now git!"

Orville, still grumbling, backed his horse out of the group and headed back toward where Kenyon crouched watching from the rocks.

As Orville passed by, Kenyon drew his Colt. "That's far enough, Orvie."

Orville stopped and quickly looked around and spotted Kenyon and his gun. He started to yell, but Kenyon cut him short.

"You make one sound, *gordo*, and it'll be your last one. Get off your horse."

Orville dismounted.

"Turn around."

Orville responded.

Kenyon rapped him alongside the head with the Colt's black barrel. Orville dropped straight down like a nugget. Turning his attention back to Riley and the remaining three Hagans, Kenyon moved to a vantage point overlooking a familiar scene.

Riley was on the ground without his pants with Bronco holding his arms and Carl pinning his legs down. Zeke once again stood over the kid with a knife in his hand.

"Well, kid, looks like it's time for a voice change, only this time you ain't got that stranger around to help you."

"I wouldn't count on it," Kenyon said.

Zeke spun around angrily.

"Hold it," Kenyon said as Carl reached for his gun.

Carl continued his movement.

As soon as Carl let loose of Riley's legs, Riley kicked hard, catching Carl in the elbow and causing him to drop the gun he'd just cleared out of his holster.

Bronco let Riley's arms go and went for his gun. Kenyon's Colt fired once, and Bronco fell over backwards with an ugly hole in the upper part of his shoulder.

Zeke yelled. "Orville!"

"I believe he's takin' a siesta," Kenyon said. "Now drop the knife and don't make any foolish moves."

Riley leaped to his feet as Zeke dropped the knife. He aimed a well-directed kick that caught Zeke in the crotch with the toe of his boot. "You sonofabitch!"

he shouted, as Zeke crumpled to the ground. "All you ever think about is cuttin' off my nuts. Well, now you've got a pair of your own that'll keep your thoughts occupied fer a spell."

"You're giving Zeke a little too much credit, Riley. I doubt that he's got much to think with at all."

"Boy, am I glad to see you!" Riley exclaimed, pulling on his pants. "How'd you find out where I was?"

"I just followed the crowd," Kenyon replied.

Carl got up holding his elbow and moved over next to Bronco, who lay unconscious on the ground. "If I don't git Bronco to the doctor, he's gonna die."

"It might teach him a lesson," Kenyon said. "You Hagans must be loose between the ears. Seems you don't learn easy."

"Can I get him to the doc?" Carl asked.

"Yeah," Kenyon replied slowly, "I guess three out of four will give the doctor a good day's work. But hear me out, Hagan. You and these dim-witted brothers of yours had better give up the idea of castratin' young Riley here. Otherwise it's going to run into a costly operation for all of you. This time it was just a shoulder wound, a pair of cracked wavos, and a lump on the head. Next time, I'll have to kill one of you."

"Mister," Carl said, his voice low and filled with anger, *"when,"* and he emphasized the word, "we come lookin' again, it won't be just for the kid. You'd better be keepin' an eye open over your shoulder 'cause there'll be a Hagan on your tail from now on."

"Get your horse, Riley, and pick mine up. He's up in those rocks. Pick up Orville's gun while you're up there. I'll keep an eye on these three till you get back."

Riley mounted the pinto and did as he was told. He returned shortly leading Kenyon's big gelding. "Shall we scatter their horses again?"

"No," Kenyon answered. "Carl here wants to get brother Bronco into town. I don't know what Zeke here's going to do. He sure can't straddle a horse, but then that ain't our problem. Just pick up their guns. We're headin' for California."

Riley started to comment on the destination California, but he caught Kenyon's don't-say-a-word expression and decided against it. After they'd ridden west for a ways, he spoke.

"Are we really headin' for California?"

"No," Kenyon said, abruptly turning north, "we're headin' for Phoenix. I just thought it might confuse the four brothers back there, at least for awhile."

"What'll I do with Orville's gun?" Riley asked, holding up the gun belt.

"Take your choice. You've got four to choose from. Then I'll toss the others away. You said you wanted a gun to learn to use. Now you've got one. Course I wouldn't choose Orville's gun belt if I was you. It looks like a cinch for a fat mare."

Riley burst out laughing. When he finally stopped, there was a serious expression on his face as he looked at Kenyon. "I don't know how to pay you back, Kenyon. This is the third time you've stepped in and saved me from either gettin' cut up or shot up."

"Who's countin'?" Kenyon said. "Listen, Kid, as soon as you learn how to use that hog leg you've got there, you'll be able to take care of yourself, and you won't need me."

"Think so?" Riley asked.

"Honest Injun," Kenyon replied.

"Yahoo!" Riley yelled, and they both laughed.

5

On the way in to Phoenix, Kenyon and Riley crossed from government land onto private land without knowing it, since there were no signs.

"Alright, let's hold it right there!" a voice commanded.

Kenyon and Riley stopped as three men rode out from behind a cluster of rocks. One of them carried a rifle.

"What's the problem?" Kenyon asked.

"We'll do the askin', sodbuster," the smallest of the three said.

"What are you two doin' on Circle T land?" This question came from a second speaker, who seemed to carry more authority than his two companions. His size added to that impression. Kenyon judged him to be over six feet tall and weighing maybe 240 pounds.

"Circle T land looks like government range," Kenyon observed. "If you don't want people on it, fence it."

The one who'd called Kenyon a sodbuster spoke again.

"Looks like this sodbuster's got a smart tongue, Hank. What you reckon we ought to do about that? Teach him a lesson?"

"You couldn't teach a constipated widow to grunt, little man," Kenyon said.

"Why you—"

"Hold it, Shorty," Hank said. Then, turning his attention back to Kenyon, he continued. "What are you two doin' around here? You ain't sodbusters."

"I'm glad you noticed," Kenyon said. "We're lookin' for work. You know anybody that could use a couple of good hands?"

"Ever work a cattle drive?" Hank asked. "We'll be goin' on one purty soon."

"Yeah," Kenyon said. "The Kid hasn't, but he learns awful fast."

"The Circle T can always use some good hands especially with all the trouble the squatters are causin'."

"You the owner?" Kenyon asked.

Hank shook his head. "I'm the foreman. Ben Terrell's the owner."

"Do we talk to Terrell about the job?" Riley asked.

"Nope! If I say you're hired, you're hired," Hank answered matter-of-factly. "You want the job?"

"We do," Kenyon replied.

"Jason, take . . . what's your names?"

"Mine's Kenyon and this is Riley."

"Take Kenyon and Riley back to the ranch and introduce them to the boss. Shorty and me will keep lookin' for squatters."

Kenyon looked at Shorty who glared back, obviously displeased that Hank had hired the two of them.

Kenyon extended an outstretched hand to Shorty. "Seein' as how we're gonna be sharing a bunkhouse, I say we shake."

"I don't shake with no worthless drifter," Shorty said, sneering.

"Up to you, short stuff," Kenyon said, straightening up again in the saddle.

Shorty turned livid with rage.

Hank grinned. "His handle is Shorty. He gets kinda touchy when people skylark with him."

"You just watch yourself," Shorty yelled as Kenyon

and the other two rode off. "Size don't mean nothin' to me."

Kenyon smiled at Jason. "Seems sort of mad, doesn't he?"

Jason grinned. "He's small but he's meaner than hell, and he's a sneaky little bastard too. Just don't turn your back on him."

The ride to the Circle T took a good half hour. The main house was a large rambling building built in the Spanish hacienda style with a red tiled roof, heavy beams, and thick adobe walls. A massive adobe arch spanned the road that led to the front of the house. Suspended beneath the arch and reaching from one side to the other was a thick heavy plank with the words "Circle T Ranch, Ben Terrell, owner" burned into it.

Jason spoke as they rode into the yard. "That little building next to the main house is where Lupita, the cook, lives with her family. To the left of it is the hands' dining room, and next to that is the bunkhouse. The other side of the bunkhouse is the barn and the corrals."

"This is quite a spread," Kenyon observed. "How many head does he run?"

"I reckon he's got at least ten thousand," Jason replied.

Kenyon whistled.

"What kind of a man is Mr. Terrell?" Riley asked.

"You can judge for yourself," Jason answered. "That's him leavin' the barn."

As they rode into the yard in front of the main house, Ben Terrell looked up.

"Are these two new hands, Jason?"

"Yes, sir," Jason replied. "Hank hired 'em while we was out on the north range."

"Come in and have a drink," Terrell said. "I'd like to talk to you."

The interior of the Terrell ranch house was just as impressive as the outside. The furniture was massive and hand-carved by artisans from Mexico. Colorful serapes hung from the walls. A large set of long horns, still attached to the stuffed head of the animal, glared down at them from above the huge walk-in fireplace. A leather wine bottle, called *la bota* by the Mexicans, hung from a wooden peg near the door.

Ben Terrell, a thick-set, barrel-chested man of medium height, moved easily across the clay-tiled floor to the liquor cabinet on the other side of the room. He struck Kenyon as a person who was used to getting exactly what he wanted. Each of his movements seemed to have been thought out purposely beforehand, giving one the feeling that Ben Terrell followed an inner direction, a kind of silent preordained set of orders that he must follow and that no one, not even himself, could countermand.

He poured two stiff drinks and hesitated. Then, looking at Riley he raised an eyebrow. "You drink, kid?"

Riley straightened up and squared his shoulders. Lowering his voice as much as possible, he replied, "I sure do. Yes, sir!"

Terrell had a hint of a grin as he poured the third drink with a heavy hand. Keeping one for himself, he offered the other two. When Kenyon and Riley had accepted his offer, he extended his hand and spoke. "I'm Ben Terrell."

"I'm Kenyon, and the drinker here is Riley."

After they'd shaken hands, Terrell spoke again. "You fellas at all tenderhearted about chasin' squatters off a man's land?"

"I usually don't like to get involved in another man's problems," Kenyon said, "but if somebody's doing something that ain't legal, I sure don't see anything wrong with making people move off your land. By the way, where does your ranch end? My partner and I were on your spread without realizing that we were trespassin'. There weren't any fences or signs posted."

"I'm tryin' to fence it as quick as I can, but when you've got fifteen thousand acres, it takes one hell of a lot of wire."

A choking sound from Riley interrupted their discussion. He flushed slightly. "Went down the wrong pipe." His voice cracked giving it the range of a nightingale. Once again he tinged a sunburned red.

Kenyon winked at Terrell. "You'd never know this kid was once plannin' to be a minister would you? I mean with his heavy drinkin' and all. . ."

Riley cleared his throat and managed a silly smile. The liquor was getting to him, but he felt sure it didn't show. As Kenyon and Terrell continued to talk, he shook his head to clear the fuzzy blur in his eyes.

"I'm havin' more trouble with them damned farmers on my north range than anywhere else right now," Terrell was saying. "There's a creek that cuts across the western part of that section, and that's where they're squattin'."

"Don't worry, Mr. Terrell," Riley cut in. "We'll run them 'quatters off the skreek . . . ah . . . seek . . . creek?"

Kenyon grinned. "I think we'd better go to the bunkhouse and store our bedrolls before he asks for another drink." He took Riley by the arm, after setting the kid's glass on the table, and directed him out the door. "I figured it was high time to get some fresh air. You notice how stuffy it was in there, Kid?"

Riley suddenly blanched of all color.

"Yeah," he said weakly, "it sure was."

Kenyon took the reins of their horses and led the animals to the hitching post in front of the bunkhouse. He untied both their bedrolls and guided Riley inside.

Jason got off his bunk to greet them.

"What's wrong with the kid? He looks like he just ate a lizard or somethin'."

"We drank some bad water on the way here," Riley volunteered, starting to regain some of his color as he sat down.

Jason waved toward four empty beds at the end of the room. "You can take one of them bunks yonder. The rest are all bein' used. The one the kid's sittin' on belongs to Hank. This one's mine. That one's Shorty's, and the others belong to the rest of the hands. You'll be meetin' them at supper time, which ought to be in about an hour. Might as well get settled in. You can turn your mounts in to that first corral near the barn. Saddles go on them rails near the gate. Anything you want to know, just holler. I got some chores to do now, so I'll see you at supper time."

Riley moved over to one of the empty lower bunks and fell into an instant sleep.

Kenyon grinned and shook his head. He dropped Riley's bedroll near the bunk and unrolled his own on the top one above the kid. Then, going outside, he led both horses to the corral and unsaddled them.

The supper was good with plenty of beef and beans and lots of hot sauce to put over it. Lupita was pleased that all the hands enjoyed eating her salsa, so she always had several large clay bowls filled with the fiery concoction placed strategically around the table.

When the meal was finished, the men made their way singly or in pairs back to the bunkhouse. One of the Mexican drovers brought out a guitar and played some beautiful ballads that told of love in old Monterrey.

Riley was back in good spirits, having had an afternoon nap and an uncommonly large meal. He and Kenyon were sitting in chairs tilted back against the whitewashed adobe wall of the bunkhouse as Shorty and another cowboy passed by in the dark.

Shorty was laughing as he related the day's activity to his friend. "And then me and Hank dragged this sodbuster out to that little shack he called his barn and made him bring out his plow horse."

"What'd you do then, tie him to the ass end?"

"Nope," Shorty answered, pleased by his friend's interest. "Hank had me shoot that critter right between the eyes."

"You mean the hoss or the sodbuster?" Shorty's friend asked.

Shorty doubled up with laughter. "That's a hot one!" he exclaimed slapping his leg. "Wait 'til Hank hears that one. I meant the horse, but I should have plugged that squatter too. Anyways, he ain't gonna be followin' no plow for the spring plantin'."

After the two men had passed in the darkness, Riley spoke, "Wasn't that small fella the one they call Shorty?"

Kenyon sighed in exasperation. "Yeah, that's the same one we saw out on the range. I can't stand that little fart."

Riley shook his head. "Me neither. I sure don't think you ought to kill a man's horse just for fun. There ain't no way that fella can feed his family come wintertime."

Kenyon sat in silence for a while before he spoke. "There might have been a good reason for it, but right now, I sure don't know what it could be."

"Well," Riley said, getting up, "I sure ain't shootin' horses for Hank or Mr. Terrell or nobody."

Kenyon got up and stretched. "Let's not take care of a problem until it comes, Kid. We need some shut-eye. Tomorrow's gonna be a long day."

From behind the blue-gray silhouetted mountains that rimmed the eastern horizon, the sun seemed to spring up with a vengeance. With penetrating arrows of golden light, it laid claim to all of the rangeland that stretched in an unbroken line to the west. Even at the early hour of five thirty, the warm rays quickly made a mist of the dewdrops and gave promise of a sweltering day that would take root long before the nooning time.

Kenyon and Riley were already in the saddle and headed toward and area that Terrell's men had started fencing several days before. When they arrived, the foreman and Shorty were just pulling up along with a wagon driven by a cowhand named Griggs. The big wagon contained numerous bails of barbed wire.

"Where's Agate?" Hank asked as he rode up.

He was referring to a cowboy who had only one eye, and it looked like a bulls-eye agate.

Kenyon shrugged.

Riley asked, "Who's Agate?"

Kenyon smiled. "Ask Shorty. Agate's one of his best friends."

"You tryin' to be funny, drifter?" Shorty asked.

Hank pressed in, ignoring Shorty's question.

"He's drivin' a wagonload of fence posts, and he should have been here by now."

"We ain't seen nobody," Riley answered, " 'cept you three."

"Make that two and a half," Kenyon added, looking straight at Shorty.

"Why you sonofabitch!" Shorty yelled.

Hank nudged his horse in between Kenyon and Shorty, averting a fight. "Alright knock it off, you two. Kenyon, you and Griggs wait here till Agate comes with the posts. Then, get started where we left off yonder by them rocks. Riley, you come with Shorty and me. We got a job to do."

"One of these days I'm gonna cut you down to size, drifter," Shorty said, as he rode past Kenyon.

"I hope it's not down to your size, Shorty. I'd hate

to have to wear my rain slicker to keep the prairie dogs from peeing on me," Kenyon replied.

Shorty was so consumed with anger, he couldn't find a worthy retort to Kenyon's remark, so he rode off surrounded by Hank's roaring laughter and a smile from Riley, who knew better than to antagonize the little man.

After several miles of silence, broken only by the clattering of horses' hoofs, Riley spoke. "Are we gonna be puttin' up fences, Hank?"

"Nope!" came the abrupt reply.

Shorty grinned as he edged up next to Riley, "We're gonna be tearin' 'em down, kid."

Riley looked perplexed. "Weren't they put up right?"

"Oh, they're right good fences," Shorty answered. Then he cackled.

"They're just in the wrong place," Hank explained. "They should be a couple of miles further to the north."

After another ten minutes of silence, they came upon a fence that stretched a half mile to the east, then bent northward disappearing beyond an outcropping of granite.

"You start here, kid. Me and Shorty will ride on beyond them rocks and start in that little valley just the other side. Throw a rope around them posts and pull 'em out."

"Yes, sir," Riley answered.

"Come on, Shorty, we got some ropin' to do too."

"Yeah," Shorty said with a chuckle. "That's my kind of ropin'."

Riley shook his head in disbelief. "I don't see nothin' so all-fired fun about ropin' a fence post," he muttered. Then he began to suspect that maybe fence posts were not what Shorty had in mind.

Riley was on his fourth fence post when a man and

a girl about nine came driving up in a wagon. Riley welcomed the chance to stop work. He smiled and removed his hat to wipe the sweatband. "Howdy," he said. "Purty hot to be so early in the day, ain't it?"

The man jumped down from the wagon and grabbed his rifle. "It's gonna be a hell of a lot hotter if you don't get them fence posts back in the ground. Now get movin'."

Riley dropped his smile and put his hat back on. "This is Mr. Terrell's land, and he said to take down this fence."

"Ben Terrell would like to have this land, but it ain't his. I homesteaded it, and I've got papers to prove it. Now put them fence posts back in their holes."

"You mean that land you're standin' on is legally yours and that Mr. Terrell is havin' me tear down fences that ain't his at all?"

The farmer's face softened a little. "You must have just started workin' for Ben Terrell not to know what kind of a skunk he is. He already owns the biggest ranch in these parts, and you'd think he'd be satisfied with that, but not Ben Terrell. He won't feel good till he runs every homesteader out of the territory. He offered me 160 dollars for my land. That's a dollar an acre, and I've built a house and a barn too."

"What about the other sodbust . . . ah . . . homesteaders? How do they feel about Terrell?"

"Well, how do you think they feel? Ever' one of them feels the way I do, but they're losin' heart. Half of 'em have already been burned out or shot or had their plow horses slaughtered."

"Pa, there's two men a-horseback comin' this way." The farmer's little daughter was standing up on the wagon seat watching Hank and Shorty approach.

The farmer levered a cartridge into the chamber of his Winchester and turned to face the two riders. "You fellas keep right on ridin' and get off my land."

"Now that ain't no way to treat a neighbor," Shorty said as he and Hank split apart, one going on each side of the farmer.

The farmer turned toward Hank who rode by the closest. As he did so, Shorty drew his gun and fired, hitting the farmer in the shoulder and causing him to drop the rifle. Shorty used his horse to ram the farmer in the back.

The farmer staggered against the wagon as his young daughter screamed at Shorty to stop it. "You quit it, you hear!" She began sobbing as she started to climb down.

"You git back on that seat and stay there lessen you want your bottom warmed," Shorty yelled.

The young girl stopped and looked at her father; the tears were still streaming down her cheeks. He nodded toward the wagon, and she understood. Climbing back on the seat, she turned and gave Shorty a dirty look.

He ignored her and crowded his horse against the farmer again. "Now you'd best listen real close, squatter. Mr. Terrell said he didn't want you hangin' around these parts no more, and who do we find when we come ridin' up? Now the next time I squeeze this trigger, the hole ain't gonna be in your shoulder. You get my meanin'?" He forced his horse against the farmer's chest mashing him against the wagon once again. The farmer groaned in pain.

Riley shouted. "Alright, Shorty, lay off! Can't you see the man's hurt?"

Shorty wheeled his buckskin around to face Riley. "You want some of it too, kid?" He spurred the buckskin next to where Riley was standing and swung his Colt at Riley's head. Riley ducked, but the Colt's barrel caught him on the cheek and sent him falling backwards.

"That's enough, Shorty," Hank called.

"I ain't finished with him yet," Shorty yelled.

"I said that's enough!" Hank's voice carried a strong threat of physical punishment that Shorty heard and couldn't ignore. Turning to Riley, who had gotten to his feet and stood shaking his head to clear the dizziness, Hank continued speaking. "Riley, you go ahead and tear down the rest of them posts. We'll see you back at the ranch at dinnertime."

"I ain't tearin' down no posts for you nor anybody else," Riley replied.

"Then clear out. You're fired."

"I didn't figure him and that other drifter would be worth a pound of eagle crap anyhow," Shorty said. "Good riddance, I say."

As they rode off, Riley turned back to the farmer. "Let's get you into the wagon. You need a doctor to look after that shoulder."

"I'll be alright," the farmer replied, but his legs sagged before he'd completed the sentence.

Riley lifted him up into the back of the wagon and then tied his own horse to the tailgate. "Where do you live?" he asked as he took the team's reins.

"Yonder behind them big rocks," the girl answered.

Riley headed the wagon in the direction she had pointed.

A tired and very worried-looking woman came to the cabin door as she heard the team approach. Like so many other farm wives, she looked a good ten years older than her actual age. The faded dress, the worn stockings, the scuffed shoes with holes and cracks that ran the length from heel to toe—all added to the image of what years of toil in the wind and sun had done to once-soft skin. When she saw Riley driving the wagon, an expression of instant dread crossed her face. She came running out of the cabin screaming.

"Where's William?" she cried. "Oh, God, did they kill him?"

"He's been shot in the shoulder, ma'am. If you'll help me get him inside, I'll go for the doctor," Riley said.

"Oh, thank you . . . yes. Isabel, you fetch some water and fill them two big pots in the fireplace. The doctor will need hot water."

"Yessum."

It took Riley about an hour to ride into town and return with the doctor.

Sarah Baden had lost none of her worried expression as she opened the door to admit to two men. "I'm beholdin' to you, Doctor, for comin' as quick as you did."

The doctor nodded and brushed past her to William Baden's bedside. "Let's have a look at that wound." After quickly looking at the point of entry, he turned to Riley. "Help me turn him over."

Riley helped the doctor roll William onto his back. "Well, it came through clean, so I don't have to do any probing. Why don't you folks go into the other room and have a seat. I'll call you if I need help."

Sarah managed a weak smile for the first time. As she and Riley entered the big main room, she spoke. "I'll bet you could stand some food, couldn't you, son? I've never seen a young fella yet that couldn't eat somethin' no matter what time of the day it was. I've got some stew and biscuits from last night. And when you finish that, I've got some sweet potatoe pie. How does that sound to you?"

Riley's smile answered her question, but he spoke anyway. "It sure sounds good, ma'am. I am a mite hungry now that you mention it."

"What's your name, young man? I never did get a chance to thank you proper for what you done."

"My name's Riley, ma'am, Thomas . . . ah Tom Riley."

"Well, Mr. Tom Riley, I'm much obliged for all you done, and I'm beholdin' to you for helpin' my man and fetchin' the doctor. Now you just sit yourself down right here, and I'll have you some food in two shakes of a lamb's tail."

"Thank you, ma'am."

"How come you happened to be right nearby when William was shot?"

Riley explained about his former job with Ben Terrell's Circle T ranch, and how he'd been fired.

Sarah's face clouded. "I'm sorry you was fired so quick, but I ain't sorry you're not workin' for the Circle T no more. That's a bad outfit. They're tryin' to run all of us little farmers out so that Ben Terrell can drive cattle from one end of the country to the other without leavin' his own range. What are you gonna do now?" she asked, placing a large cut of pie in front of Riley.

He couldn't resist taking a big bite first and then answering her with his mouth full. "I don't rightly know. My friend Kenyon is still workin' for Terrell 'cause he don't know I quit. I'll see him tonight when I go back to pick up my stuff."

The doctor came in. "I'd sure appreciate a cup of water, Mrs. Baden." When that was supplied, he drank it and wiped his brows before speaking again. "Your husband's going to be alright. It'll be quite some time before he can do a good day's work, and that shoulder will never be the same again, but he'll be okay. I left some bandages in on your dresser top. You change it every day or so. I'll come back out in about a week."

"How much do I owe you, Doctor?"

"Forget it. I'll add it on to what Ben Terrell owes me. The boy here tells me it was one of the Circle T's outfit that shot your husband, so I reckon it's only fair that they pay." With that he put on his hat and left.

Riley stood up. "Is there anything you'd like me to do, ma'am?"

"If you'd give Isabel a hand out yonder unhitchin' the team, I'd be obliged."

"Yes, ma'am."

Riley went out and took the reins from Isabel's small hands. "Let me do that for you, young lady."

Isabel managed a worried smile. "Is my pa gonna be alright?"

"Why, heckfire yeah. He's a tough man, that daddy of yours."

When he had unhitched the team, he put the horses in the small corral and hung the harness on two wooden pegs driven into the adobe blocks that formed the three walls of the lean-to. Then he noticed that several of the upright posts had held the horizontal logs in place for the corral were leaning out of kilter. Closer inspection showed that they had been pulled out and had just been dropped back into their holes without being firmed up with dirt tamped down around their bases. Riley figured that Mr. Baden had probably been working on them just before he had driven the wagon out to chase Riley off his property. Riley figured the least he could do was to repair the Baden corral, so he set to work.

Mrs. Baden came out of the house. "You don't have to do that, Tom. I'll take care of it."

"I'd like to help you, ma'am, if you don't mind. I ain't been on a farm for quite a spell, and it's kinda nice to be on one again. How's Mr. Baden?"

"He's sleepin' now, so I thought I'd git out here and not wake him up a-bangin' around in the kitchen."

Riley looked up from his work. "Ain't none of the homesteaders ever gone to the sheriff about what Terrell's a-doin'? It seems to be mighty illegal . . . his hired hands a-shootin' and killin' people and burnin' their homes."

"It is illegal, and we have gone to the sheriff, but Ed Wallace ain't much of a lawman. He says it's just our word against Ben Terrell's. He says he'd have to catch Terrell's hired hands in the act before he could arrest them. Since most of the shootin's and burnin's have been at night, and Sheriff Wallace goes off duty at supper time, there ain't much chance that he'll ever catch anything but indigestion."

"Well, it seems to me that if ever'body got together and got some guns, they could stop Terrell's men with a little lead."

Sarah Baden shook her head. "We tried that, but ever'body's spread out so much, it's too hard to cover all the farms. Terrell's men would hit one place, and by the time all the farmers got together and rode over there, his men would shoot up another farm five miles away."

"It just ain't right," Riley said as he firmed up the last post. "Maybe my friend Kenyon can think of a way to stop Terrell once he finds out what he's a-doin'."

"I don't think your friend will want to take on Ben Terrell. He's too powerful in these parts. Besides, this friend of yours doesn't have a stake in the homesteader's problems."

Riley looked at Sarah's tired face. It reminded him of the way his mother used to look. "Kenyon's the best man I've ever met. He'll fight for what he believes is right whether he has a stake in it or not. You'll see."

As he looked around the Baden homestead, his jaw muscles tightened in anger. These people deserved the right to own and operate their farm without someone riding roughshod over them. Terrell had to be stopped. That was certain.

"I'd best be goin' now, Miz Baden. I still have to go out to Terrell's and git my bedroll."

"Let me fix you some food 'fore you go. You've done a nice piece of work here."

Riley's stomach was at the growling stage again, but he knew the Badens were short on food.

"No, thank you, ma'am. I ain't hungry. I've got to go meet my friend, Kenyon. You take care now. Ever'-thing's gonna be changin' soon and . . . well . . . you folks will be alright. So long, ma'am. Bye, Isabel."

As Riley rode out, young Isabel waved and threw him a kiss. He smiled and waved back. He wondered why the good people of the world always seemed to be getting the short end of everything and the bad ones seemed to do so well. Maybe Kenyon could explain it.

6

KENYON LOOKED FOR RILEY WHEN HE RODE in, but the Kid wasn't back yet, apparently. He asked several of the other hands if they had seen him, but they all said no. He decided that since it was supper time, he'd go in and eat. Riley never missed a meal, so he was bound to show up at the cowhands' dining room.

Kenyon had finished eating his supper and was heading back to the corral to see if the pinto was there when he saw Riley come flying through the bunkhouse doorway and land in the dirt outside. An instant later Shorty stepped out and kicked Riley in the rear just as he was getting up. Riley went down again. Shorty raised his foot to bring it down on the back of Riley's head. Kenyon drew his Colt and fired. The slug caught the heel of Shorty's boot and sent him spinning off balance. He fell to the earth near Riley.

Riley seized his opportunity and drove a bony fist into Shorty's face before the little man could get to his feet.

Kenyon's shot brought most of Terrell's men out of the bunkhouse to watch the fight. Hank was just coming out of the main house when he spotted the two men on the ground. He sauntered over at an easy pace. He had no particular reason to separate the men. After all, he considered a good fight the highlight of his day. When he discovered it was Riley, his face beamed.

Two of the cowhands decided that Riley was no match for Shorty, so they started to break it up. Hank spoke: "Let 'em be!"

"Shorty'll kill him," one of the men said.

"He deserves what he's gonna get. I told that kid he was fired this mornin', and here he is still hangin' around."

Kenyon stepped in and grabbed Shorty's pants at the belt line and lifted him off Riley's prostrate form.

"I said leave 'em alone," Hank bellowed.

Kenyon, still holding Shorty by the pants and belt, grabbed the little man by the shirt collar with his left hand and spun in a fast circle letting Shorty go just at the peak of his momentum. Shorty hit Hank full in the stomach with his head and shoulders knocking the wind out of the beefy foreman and sending both of them to the ground.

Riley was just getting to his feet when Kenyon spoke. "Get our bedrolls, Kid, and put them on our horses." Riley hurried into the bunkhouse to carry out Kenyon's order.

Shorty pulled himself off Hank's gasping body and leaped at Kenyon with the fury of a loco bull.

"You sonofabitch!" he screamed.

Kenyon timed his swing and caught Shorty flush on the jaw with a short but powerful right cross.

Shorty dropped like he'd been struck by lightning.

Hank's breath had returned enough for him to call out. "Get him!"

Kenyon drew his Colt once again but didn't fire. The men stopped instantly. There's something about staring down the muzzle of a loaded gun that takes the starch out of most men's legs. Terrell's bunch were no exceptions.

Kenyon eyed them cooly. "I don't mind taking you jaspers on one at a time, but I do hate crowds. Now just take it easy, and the Kid and I will ride out peaceful like, and nobody'll get hurt."

One of the men started to move, and Kenyon glanced in his direction. "You don't want an extra belly button, do you fella?"

The cowpoke swallowed dryly and shook his head. "Then stand still!" Kenyon ordered.

Riley emerged and quickly tied the bedrolls behind the saddles of their horses. He mounted his and led Kenyon's dun to where his friend was standing.

"You fellas pitch your guns over there by that hitchin' post . . . and do be careful," Kenyon said.

They did as he ordered. Kenyon mounted up, and as they rode out, Hank yelled at them. "Next time we meet, there's gonna be trouble, Kenyon!"

After they'd ridden hard for a ways, they eased up and let their horses breathe. Kenyon looked at Riley and shook his head, sighing heavily. "What in the hell did you do to Shorty, crap in his saddle bags?"

Riley chuckled. "I didn't do nothin' to him." Then he related the morning's experience and how Shorty had hit him in the face with his gun barrel.

Kenyon listened intently. When Riley had finished telling the story he spoke.

"Then these people, like that man you helped, aren't squatters after all," he said softly. "Terrell's been havin' us do his dirty work for him."

"That's right," Riley answered, "but Terrell's got fifteen thousand acres now. Why in the world would he want more for?"

"That's what makes kings," Kenyon replied. "They're not satisfied till they've stolen all the land and forced everyone to knuckle under and come crawlin' on their knees."

"Well, I'm sure glad I ain't part of that bunch no more," Riley said. "I just wished I'd slugged Shorty a little harder, that's all!"

Kenyon grinned. "I took care of that for you, Kid. I think I might have broken the little fart's jaw. Something kind of crunched when I hit him."

"Yahoo!" Riley hooted. "I sure wish I'd have done that."

They rode along in silence for a few minutes.

"Where are we going now?" Riley asked.

"Well, Kid, I'll leave that up to you. The way I figure it, we can ride out of here and not look back, or we can stick around and see what's gonna happen."

Riley thought for a while before answering. "If we stay here, we prob'bly won't like what we see, so I figure leavin' would be a lot safer."

"More than likely," Kenyon agreed.

"But then, ding bust it, these are just little folks a-bein' pushed around by Terrell and Hank and Shorty and the rest of them no accounts. It just ain't fair," Riley said.

He looked over at Kenyon and studied his face, hoping for guidance, but the face showed nothing of his friend's inner thoughts.

"Well, heckfire," he continued. "I say we stay. I figure them homesteaders need some help more than we need to move on."

"Sounds right to me," Kenyon answered, turning his horse off the road. "I think we'd better find a good spot to camp for the night. We'll go back into town tomorrow and see if we can locate another job."

"Why don't we go in tonight," Riley asked. "I'm sure hungry."

"No point payin' for a bed when we can sleep out here," Kenyon replied. "There should be some jerky and hardtack in my saddle bags."

"That ain't exactly what I call a full-up supper," Riley complained.

"What do you want to do, develop a fat belly like those bankers in town?" Kenyon asked.

Riley shrugged. "At least I could hold my pants up," he grumbled.

Kenyon laughed.

"It's easy for you to laugh. You ate your supper. All I got was a big helpin' of fists and boots."

"It toughens you, Kid. That's what helps forge you into the strong silent type that ladies cotton to."

"I'd druther be weak and stuffed full," Riley commented.

"I'll make a fire. At least we can have some hot coffee. That is if you'll get the water. I saw a little creek just beyond those rocks," Kenyon said. "We've only got about two minutes of light left, so you'd better hurry or you'll bring back a pot full of frogs."

Riley was gone for a while and then came back with the coffee water. "I thought I heard somethin' in them bushes out there. You don't reckon them Hagans are still trackin' us do you?"

Kenyon smiled as Riley set the pot on the fire he'd just built. "You can't tell about those jaspers. They could break in on us any time."

Riley glanced over his shoulder nervously. "Don't you reckon they're on a trail to California? That's where you told 'em we was goin'."

"I'd like to think so, but I wouldn't count on it. They're a pretty dumb bunch, but I'm afraid they may have a little more savvy than that."

7

"WHO'S THAT LONG, TALL, DRINK OF WAter?" Hank asked as Brownlee, the storekeeper, finished loading a keg of nails into Helen's buckboard and then stood watching as she drove away.

"That's Helen Tilsbury, and don't let the fact that she's raw-boned and gray-haired fool you. She's a tough old bird. She knows exactly what she wants and she won't take no for an answer," Brownlee said smiling.

"Yeah, I know what you mean. I seen her before, but it was dark and I couldn't get a look at her face. She don't scare easy; that's for sure."

Helen pulled her buckboard off the main road and took the lightly rutted trail to her homestead, 160 acres of semi-arid gentle slopes that tapered into flatlands. The land, twenty years before, had been covered with perennial grasses. Now, the grasses were being replaced by the invasive mesquite, and tarbushes, and the drab-hued creosote.

She stopped the buckboard in front of the partially completed cow shed and took off the good bonnet she had worn into town. She reached under the seat, took out an old bonnet and an apron she had hidden there, and put them on. Readjusting her bun so the bonnet would slip forward more and give extra protection to her eyes, she raised a tan weathered hand to block the sun's rays and looked up toward the ridgepole outlined against the crisp blue sky. "Today I'm gonna nail you down," she said. Then, stepping down to the ground, she grabbed a hammer, broke open the top of the nail keg, and shoved a handful of nails into the pocket of her apron. She set an empty box on the bed of the buckboard, then crawled up and leaned it against the upright support for the ridgepole. Holding the hammer in one hand and clutching the upright post with the other, she carefully stood on top of the box and began to trail the ridgepole into place. After several successful swings with her hammer, she accidently whacked one thumb and let out a yelp of pain. The horse started moving forward. Helen grabbed onto the ridgepole as the box she was standing on fell to the ground.

"Whoa! Bessie, dern your hide. Whoa!"

The horse continued to move until the buckboard was no longer underneath her.

"Bessie, git back here, you boneheaded jackass! Come back here! Bessie!"

Kenyon heard Helen's yell from the main road and stopped. "Sounds like someone's in trouble, Kid. Let's take a look."

As he and Riley rounded the slight bend in the trail, they could see Helen hanging from the ridgepole, kicking wildly. The rear of the buckboard was just out of reach. Her dress was caught on the side of the post, which held it up on one side, exposing her long bloomers and high-buttoned shoes.

Kenyon kicked the line-back into a gallop and yelled, "Hold on, ma'am!"

Pulling up underneath Helen, he placed a strong arm around her waist. "You can let go now, ma'am. I've got you."

"Turn your head, young man. I ain't in the habit of havin' my bloomers a-flappin' fer the whole blamed world to see."

Kenyon grinned; then he turned his head and lowered her gently to the ground.

After she had smoothed out her dress and regained her composure, she cleared her throat and spoke. "I'm . . . ah . . . certainly beholdin' to you fer gittin' me down offen that fool pole. That dumb horse's got a mind of her own at times. She walked right out from under me, and me yellin' all the time fer her to stop."

Kenyon and Riley both laughed. Then Riley spoke. "It looks like you need a hand, ma'am. My pardner and I will put that up for you."

"Now, that's right neighborly of you. You fellas live around here?"

"Well, we did 'til yesterday. Then Terrell fired us," Riley said grinning.

Helen's face hardened. "So you worked for Terrell, did you."

Kenyon could hear the disgust in Helen's voice. "We did 'til we found out how he was treatin' his neighbors," he answered.

Her expression softened. "So you're out of work now, are you?"

"Yes, ma'am," Riley said, dismounting. "You know of anybody that could use two good men?"

"Two good men, huh?" There was a twinkle in Helen's eye as she gave Riley a close appraisal. Then she turned her attention to Kenyon. Now here's a real man, she thought. He looks like he could take on a grizzly with a handful of pebbles and come out wearin' a fur coat. "Let me do a little thinkin' on that. If you fellas will fix that ridgepole fer me, I'll git some vittles ready fer the noonday meal. Then we'll talk about maybe findin' you some work. How does that sound?"

"Sounds jim-dandy to me, ma'am," Riley said, rolling up his sleeves.

"How about you?" she asked, looking pointedly at Kenyon.

He dismounted and smiled at Helen. "Sounds fine, Miz. . ."

"Tilsbury—Helen Tilsbury, and you're. . . ?"

"I'm Kenyon and this strappin' bruiser is Thomas Jefferson Riley."

"Well I do declare . . . Thomas Jefferson Riley! Now that's what I call a noble-soundin' name."

"It's fitting," Kenyon said grinning.

"Well, I'll let you boys . . . ah . . . *men* . . . git to work, and I'll git that fire goin'."

After she had gone into the house, he turned to Riley. "When you first meet somebody, Kid, don't give 'em so much information. Someday it just might get you shot before you have a chance to explain what you're talkin' about."

"What did I say?" Riley asked, bewilderment showing on his face.

"Your comment about our workin' for Ben Terrell. It's not a good idea to let folks know right away that we worked for an hombre like that."

"Yeah, I reckon I wasn't thankin'," he said, a little embarrassed.

They set to work and got Helen's ridgepole nailed into place and the rafters attached to the ridgepole. Then, as they started to put the cut squares of buffalo-grass sod onto the roof rafters, Helen yelled from her cabin.

"Come and git it!"

Riley was off like a shot. He didn't even stop at the wash bucket Helen had put out for them; he headed straight for the door.

Kenyon called. "Riley, give me a hand here for a second, will you?"

Riley stopped, surprised, and walked back to where Kenyon was standing.

"Yeah?"

Kenyon lowered his voice. "I think she would be a

little disappointed if we went in without washin' up. Women are kinda particular about that. Know what I mean?"

Riley's ears took on a red tone. "Yeah! I guess I just wasn't thankin' again. I'm sure glad you caught me in time."

The two of them walked to the wash bucket together.

After they had sat down and Helen had served them, she spoke.

"If you fellas are out of a job, I can give you one if you don't mind low pay fer awhile. I can feed you well and maybe give you enough fer a decent pair of pants fer young Riley here. I'm a little short on hard money, but I got some friends comin' out here fer a meetin' this afternoon and between all us we oughta be able to pay you some wages."

"I don't see any cattle," Kenyon said. "I'm a cowpoke by trade, so I'd be kind of useless doin' farm work."

"Ain't nothin' mysterious about farm work," Helen said. "If there was, *I* wouldn't be able to do it."

Riley grinned with a mouthful of potatoes partly showing. "I kin show you ever'thing you need to know, Kenyon. There ain't *nothin'* about farmin' that I don't know about."

"I'm glad to hear that," Kenyon mumbled. "What have you got in mind, Miz Tilsbury?"

"Well," she said, raising her eyebrows at them, "you both know what kind of a man Ben Terrell is and what he's done to the homesteaders hereabouts."

"Yes, ma'am," Riley said. "I seen what he done firsthand."

"Well, he paid me a visit last night."

"Ben Terrell did?" Kenyon asked.

"Not Ben himself, just that buzzard bait he's got workin' fer him, that big ugly foreman and some of them other coyotes. They came through after dark and yelled a lot of threats and tore up my garden. Then, after promisin' what they'd do to me and my place the next time they came a-callin', they fired a few shots and left.''

"Why did he choose you to pick on?" Riley asked as anger began to tighten his face. "Prob'bly 'cause you ain't got a man to carry a gun for you."

"Ben Terrell gave a whole passel of us widows train tickets and promised us a hundred dollars apiece to come out here and homestead gov'ment property. Then, we're suppose to sign it over to him . . . only I changed my mind. I'm keepin' my homestead and there are several more who feel the same way. We want to try and talk the others into joinin' us. Our homestead boundaries touch each other, so we could, if ever'body agrees, make it into one big spread of nearly two thousand acres."

"That's a mighty big farm," Riley said, mopping up the last of the gravy from his plate with a biscuit.

"That's true," she agreed. "Bigger then any I've ever lived on. I figured if you boys was to start workin', the first thang we'd have you do, is put up some bobbed wire, so we could keep them danged cattle of his off our property."

"It sounds good to me, ma'am. Could I have a piece of one of them cakes?" Riley asked.

Helen smiled and cut a couple pieces of cake, "And you, Kenyon, are you willin' to stay?"

"Yeah, I need to hang my hat in one place for awhile."

Helen rose. "Why don't you fellas each take a piece of cake out with you, and when you're finished eatin' it, put a roof on that little cow shed out there 'cause that's where you'll be beddin' down. I've got to git this place cleaned up cause them women will be here directly."

As they got up to leave, she put her hand on Kenyon's arm. "I'd like you boys to be in on the meetin'. Then they could hear firsthand what Terrell's been up to."

The roof was half finished when the first buckboard pulled up in front of Helen's cabin. Soon there were several others, each with two or three women in it. The women sat on benches Helen had provided for some serious talking. They ate a crumb cake and drank coffee.

Kenyon looked at the crowd of females. "Let's stay back here out of sight 'til they start the meetin'. Otherwise, they'll talk our legs off."

"Yeah," Riley agreed. "I ain't much good at talkin' around women . . . 'specially a whole herd of 'em."

"Well," Helen said, smiling at her guests, "I'm mighty pleased ever'body could come. Sorry I couldn't have this meetin' inside but it's tighter than a bug's ear in there. I've got some things to be said, and it's best to say 'em out here where we can see what we're talkin' about. Now I know that all of you women are widows like I am, and you ain't got nobody to speak up for you or fight for you. I know that all of you came out here because Ben Terrell paid your coach fare and promised you a hundred dollars if you'd homestead a piece of ground and then turn it over to him. Well, I for one ain't givin' my place to Ben Terrell or nobody else."

"That's not the ethical, Christian thing to do, Mrs. Tilsbury. You made a promise to Mr. Terrell, and you accepted his money for the train ride."

Helen stared at the speaker, a small, moon-faced woman with the type of white skin that was always protected from the sun by a bonnet or a parasol. "I don't believe I know you ma'am," she said.

"That's Clara Mae Hodges. She just came in town about a week ago," Lydia Nofzigger said.

"I'd be obliged if you called me Helen, Clara Mae," Helen said calmly. "The other sounds too formal-like. It's plain to see that you don't know nothin' about Ben Terrell or what he's been doin' out here."

Clara Mae shook her head. "Mrs. Babcott and some of the other ladies have been telling me some very upsetting things about him on our ride out here, but I really don't see that what kind of man Mr. Terrell is, has anything to do with our obligation to him. We made a promise to turn the land over to him before we accepted his offer. I just think it's unethical and maybe even illegal to break our promises."

"It's nothing of the sort," Lydia countered. "The land is legally ours. The government says so."

"That's right," Alpha Babcott added, "and the United States government is bigger than Ben Terrell by a dern sight. That's what I have to say."

Some of the other women murmured in agreement.

"Well, I just don't know," Clara Mae said.

Helen bit a loose piece of skin on her chapped lip. "Well, in case the others left somethin' out, I'll just tell you myself what kind of sidewinder we're dealin' with here, and then you tell me if you still feel the same way. Ben Terrell's men have either killed or crippled half a dozen homesteaders around here. Not only that, but they've shot their plow horses, killed their stock, and burned down their barns." Clara Mae started to interrupt her, but Helen continued. "Now it seems to me, Miz Hodges, you've been a-doin' a lot of talkin' about loyalty and ethics and all, and I ask you. Why would an ethical man do that to his neighbors?" Without waiting for an answer, Helen continued. "And the answer is, Ben Terrell and his Circle T don't know the meanin' of the word ethical, nor any other kind of right and wrong, and they don't want neighbors neither, at least not our kind of neighbors."

"But!" Clara Mae interrupted.

"I heard your piece," Helen continued, glaring hard at Clara Mae. "Now you hear me out." Dealing with fools had never been one of Helen's virtues, and this woman was straining what little patience she had. "Terrell owns fifteen thousand acres of land in these parts, and he grazes his cows on thousands of acres that ain't his at all. It's gov'ment land, and now it's bein' opened up, legal and fair, to farm folks like us who want to own a piece of ground for themselves. What I'm gettin' to is this," Helen said, her voice increasing in volume. "I rode over to see Ben Terrell yesterday, and I told him I'm gonna keep my homestead. I said I'd pay him back for the train fare, but I homesteaded the land, and I aim to keep it. Now I know that some of you feel as I do, so if you want to join me, we'll fight this together if we have to."

"Well I, for one, feel the same way Helen does," Alpha said. "How about the rest of you?"

Till now Bertha Rees had sat quietly listening to the others without comment. Now she spoke up. "I've been out here long enough to know that what Helen's saying about Ben Terrell is true, but up to this point nobody's bothered any of us widows. I just don't know, Helen."

"Honey, if I was as young and pretty as you and a couple of others here, I wouldn't worry about any man botherin' me 'less he was comin' a-courtin'," Alpha said.

"Thirty-four isn't exactly a spring chicken," Bertha replied.

"It seems almost diaper stage to me," Alpha said. "I can't remember when I was thirty-four—it's been so long."

"Well, Ben Terrell ain't bothered us because we was

doin' exactly what he wanted us to do," Helen said. "But turnin' a blind eye to the bad bein' done around you is no decent way to live. It makes a body feel small and ashamed." Then, softening her expression and her voice, she continued. "Some of you are in a little different situation than the rest of us. You're still young enough to get a man and start fresh buildin' a life together. The rest of us cain't do that. For us this is kinda the last stand. It's either this or the poor farm."

"Mr. Terrell is going to be awfully mad—isn't he?—if we all decide to stay put and not sell him our land?" Fanny Whitcomb asked in her high thin voice. "Won't he send some of his men around to cause some trouble for us?"

Helen smiled. "He's already done that. Last night he sent some of his boys over to raise a little cain. They rode around and fired a few shots into the air tryin' to scare me, buy it didn't do no good. All they done was trample down my garden, but it'll grow again."

"I'm with Helen and Alpha," Lydia said with power. "I say we vote!"

"How come we only have women here, Helen?" Fanny Whitcomb asked, ignoring Lydia's pressure. "There are some men homesteaders that haven't been shot. Why aren't they and their families here?"

"The problems we're discussin', Fanny, is whether or not all of us *widows* can git together and agree on a plan of action. Once we do that we can show a united front to the rest of them homesteaders, and it'll make it easier to git 'em to stand up with us against Terrell. *Besides,* there ain't just women here. I'd like you ladies to meet Kenyon and Thomas Jefferson Riley. They worked fer Ben Terrell—fer awhile. Then, they found out what kind of cow chip they was workin' fer and they quit. Listen to what they have to say. Tell 'em what you told me, boys!''

The women all turned and gazed at Kenyon and Riley. There were murmurs of astonishment that Helen had managed to get two young men to work for her when they all knew that she, like they themselves, had little money to spare.

Riley looked down at his boots and kicked at a clod of dirt. Alpha smiled and spoke. "How about you, Tommy? What did Terrell have you doin'?"

"I was supposed to tear down some fences and then put 'em up somewheres else," Riley said still looking at the ground.

"What was so bad about that?" Fanny asked.

"Them fences didn't belong to Mr. Terrell," Riley said. Then he went on to explain what had happened at the Baden homestead—how William Baden had been shot, how Riley had decided to quit right there on the spot and take Mr. Baden back to his house.

"Well, God bless you, son. You sure done the right thing," Alpha said.

Riley had begun to warm up to the friendly response he was getting, so he continued the story while looking directly into the women's faces and told them how Kenyon had saved him from a beating at the hands of Shorty when he had gone back to the Circle T to pick up his gear.

Kenyon didn't say anything, but from the hint of a smile on his face, it was evident he was enjoying watching Riley blossom into a speaker.

"As you can see, these boys are worth keepin! They're good hands," Helen said. "If we can all pay a little bit each month, they'll do a lot of work that can't be done by us. They can string some bobbed wire around the whole spread to keep Terrell's cattle out."

"Sounds good to me," Fanny said. "Let's vote on it!"

"Now just a minute here," Clara Mae said. "If Mr. Terrell's men have been shooting homesteaders, why hasn't the sheriff been sent for? If he's doing something illegal, the sheriff should punish him for it."

"That sheriff's about as useful as tits on a boar," Helen said, glaring at Clara Mae. "I happened to be over at the Dawson's right after they was shot up by the Circle T riders. One of Dawson's sons went in and told that jackass Ed Wallace about what had happened. It was three days before he rode out to the farm to see for himself. He's got the backbone of a piss ant."

"Terrell's got him bought and paid for," Lydia added.

"Then what can we do?" Clara Mae asked.

Helen rolled her eyes upwards. "For God's sake, woman, that's what we're talkin' about. We stick together and stand as a united group! Then we git them other farmers that are able to stand up and carry a gun, and we fight Terrell on his own ground."

Alpha spoke again. "I say let's keep our land. It's legally owned, and besides, the Circle T lays claim to too blamed many acres anyways. I say Ben Terrell's gotten too big for his britches and ought to be taken down a notch or two. I think Helen and Lydia and me are the ones to do it. Any of you gals want to join us, or are you all gonna take your hunderd dollars and hightail it back to wherever you came from?"

"Well, as much as I agree with what you're saying, I wouldn't want to live in this place for a day longer than it takes me to get the papers on the land, then turn around and sell it," Emma Scraton said. "I'm not as hardy as I used to be. I was raised in an area that's green the year around. I just can't take this dry air and constant dust and lack of water. This place will take ten years off your lives if you stay here."

Helen winked at Alpha. "That would mean I'll only live to be 105. Guess I'd better pack my bags."

The women laughed. Alpha studied Emma's full unlined face. "You say you agree with what we've been talking about, but you don't want to stay here yourself?"

"That's right?"

"Don't you have the land that borders Fanny Whitcomb's place?"

"Yes I do. I'm on the north side of her property."

"What's your water situation?"

"I got a well."

"A good one?"

"Oh . . . it will do."

"Well, why don't you sell your place to us for one hunderd dollars 'stead of to Ben Terrell? Then you can git back to them green trees of yourn 'fore you dry up," Alpha said.

Emma smiled, "I'm willing to do that, especially if I can give Mr. Terrell back the money for the train ride he paid for."

"Sounds like to me Alpha and Emma have come up with somethin' pretty good here," Helen said. "Would you ladies consider chippin' in about ten or fifteen dollars apiece so we can buy Emma's land?"

"I don't have fifteen dollars," Mary Bonesteel said. "And even if I did have it, and we bought Emma's homestead, who would take care of it?"

"These two young men right here," Helen said.

"That's a pretty big farm to work," Maggie Gilmore said.

"We'll manage alright," Helen added. "The main thing is, who's for stayin'?"

"Count me in," Fanny replied.

"Me too," Lydia added.

When the final count was taken, eight women stood united against Ben Terrell's Circle T, two ladies decided against joining the others, and two were undecided as yet. Helen considered the meeting a smacking success.

Plans were made for the eight women to get together and have a cabin raising for each of them that didn't have herself a house to live in. They decided to pool their labor and their money. They'd buy barbed wire and have Kenyon and Riley put up fences; then, they could get down to the serious job of farming the land.

As the women climbed back aboard the wagons, Alpha turned back to Helen and spoke. "We done somethin' good here today, Helen. 'Fore you know it, there'll be farmers comin' to town by the dozen. Maybe Ben Terrell will realize then that there's room here for ever'body, farmers and cattlemen alike."

"I hope so, Alpha. I'm gettin' too old to keep movin' on. This is where I want to plant my roots."

Alpha grinned. "Me too. See you tomorrow."

Helen stood for a long time watching the wagons leave. When they were out of sight she started picking up the cake plates and coffee cups. Then she turned and spoke to Kenyon.

"Well, what do you think? You reckon we've got a chance against Terrell?"

Kenyon started helping pick up the cups while Riley ate the crumbs from the plates as he gathered them together. "I think you'll do alright. You've got the law on your side, and I don't mean Ed Wallace. We'll send for the U.S. marshal. That should take the wind out of Terrell's sails for a while."

8

THE SUN THRUST ITS BRAZEN YELLOW DOME through a wisp of clouds clinging stubbornly to the eastern peaks of the mountain range that pierced the sky behind Helen's homestead. A flock of lean multicolored chickens pecked in the thin band of golden light that warmed the decomposed granite pebbles which here and there hid a treasured wild seed or two.

Kenyon stood in the front yard and surveyed Helen's land. The garden that Hank and his friends had trampled into a pile of clods and crushed plants was at one side of the small adobe house. On the other side and stretching off at a forty-five-degree angle to join the corral was the lean-to shed that he and Riley had put a sod roof on yesterday. The boulder directly behind the shed, which served as the structure's back wall, offered protection from most of the wind. When the rains came, however, Kenyon knew that sheets of water would cascade down the rock's smooth face and the sod roof would let the rain pour in once the earth became saturated. The dirt floor would quickly become a quagmire. If they took out two sections of the corral fence, they could build a room with a proper roof and attach it to the shed. Helen had said that she and the Hernandez brothers had carried clay from the butte at the far end of her property. He and Riley would make more adobe bricks and build a strong room that would give them protection from both the summer's heat and the winter's cold.

He shook his head and gave an almost inaudible sigh.

"Ain't much is it?" Helen said as she walked up smiling.

"You know you're gonna have to replace the sod roof on that cowshed. That stuff is about as waterproof as cheesecloth. It's gonna take a lot of work to make this place into a farm," he said.

She cocked her head to one side and grinned. "You sound like you're ready to throw in the towel before we even git started."

Kenyon's smile broadened. "I never let hard work bother me."

"That's good," Helen said.

"Yeah, I can stand right next to it all day long."

She laughed and slapped him on the shoulder.

"I'm gonna ride into town and send a telegram to the U.S. marshal. I think he'll be mighty interested in what Terrell's doin'," Kenyon said.

"I'll take care of that today. It's our responsibility to notify the marshal. You boys just keep on workin'. We'll take care of Mr. Ben Terrell."

Kenyon grinned. "You sure ain't lettin' any grass grow under your feet, are you?"

Helen smiled. "Not where Ben Terrell is concerned."

Riley walked up scratching his belly. "What are we gonna do first?"

"I think we'd better make some adobe bricks and build a room onto that shed. When summer gets here, it's gonna be hotter than the hubs of hell, and the adobe will give us a cool place to sleep. That'll leave the shed Helen started completely free for the cow she ain't got."

"I'll git one. Don't you worry none about that," she said.

While Kenyon and Riley were bringing clay from the butte to make a supply of adobe bricks, Helen set out for town to send the telegram. By the time the men had a number of them drying in the sun, she had returned and had started putting her garden back into shape.

While the bricks were curing, Kenyon suggested that now was a good time for Riley to learn to use a handgun. They rode to a hill on the back side of Helen's property.

As Riley was putting cartridges into the old .44 he had taken from Orville Hagan, Kenyon reached over and placed his hand on the tip of the barrel and pushed it down.

"Your first lesson, Kid, is to not point the gun at anyone unless you intend to shoot him."

Riley turned red as he shook his head. "I'm sorry about that, Kenyon. Guess I was just concentratin' and not watchin' what I was doin'."

"You'll get it alright. Now, the first thing to remember is to squeeze the trigger. If you yank on it or jerk it, you won't be able to hit a barn. Try it."

"What'll I aim at?"

"Nothin' right now. Just get the feel of squeezin' the trigger."

Riley jerked the trigger and the .44 nearly jumped out of his hand. "Wow! That's sure got a kick to it."

Kenyon grinned. "It'll break your thumb if you don't keep it back out of the road. Now, point it at that white rock over there and remember about squeezin' the trigger."

Riley squeezed the trigger, but the .44 was swaying so much he clipped a small limb from a bush to the right of the rock. "How do you keep this danged thang from weavin' so much?"

"The trick is to have a little muscle in your arm. If the gun is too heavy for you, use both hands to hold it."

"If I did that, they'd laugh me out of ever' town from here to California." He slipped the .44 back into its holster. "I'm gonna try a fast draw."

Before Kenyon could say, "No, don't!" Riley yanked the gun, and it went off before it had cleared the holster. The bullet tore a notch out of the sole of his boot, missing his toe by a quarter of an inch. He let the gun fall back into its holster and then stood there trying to control his breathing.

Kenyon checked the urge to laugh and settled for a sly smile while he waited for Riley to quit shaking.

"I thank I'd better practice them slow shots for a spell 'fore I try any fancy fast draws and such."

Kenyon's smile grew into a broad grin. "That's a good idea, Kid. I'm glad you thought of it."

Then he and Riley burst out laughing at the same time.

The following day, after Kenyon had given Riley another shooting lesson, Helen took some money from her purse and handed it to Kenyon.

"Why don't you ride into town and see if you can find somebody who's willin' to sell a good workhorse, or even a mule if he's a strong one."

"I'll go with him. I know somethin' about plow horses," Riley said.

"You'll do no such thing. I want you to help me finish puttin' that garden in shape."

Kenyon mounted up. "I'll see you later, Farmer Riley." He grinned as he rode off.

He decided the blacksmith would be the best man to talk to about a work animal, so he reined to a halt in front of the smithy's forge and dismounted. The smith, a thick-set German named Herman Konig, was busy putting a new rim on a wagon wheel, so Kenyon stood and waited. When Herman was finished, he leaned the wheel against the wall and wiped his perspiring brow with a great, blue handkerchief.

Kenyon spoke. "Herman, I'm lookin' for a good draft animal, one that can pull a plow or a wagon without too much strain. You know where I might find such an animal?"

"Ya. You vant mule or horse?"

"Whichever is cheaper," Kenyon answered.

"I got both—same price. Family leave animals to pay for funeral."

"Hey, smitty, you got them wagon wheels done yet? Mr. Terrell's gonna be awful sore if he don't—well, lookey who's here. Hello, Kenyon. I thought you'd be headin' for parts unknown by now."

Kenyon turned and saw one-eyed Agate staring at him. "When I have a reason for goin', I'll go."

"I'll put veels on vagon right now," Herman replied. "Just a minute and I show you good plow horse," Herman said over his shoulder to Kenyon as he picked up the wheel he'd just repaired and began greasing the inside of the hub.

Agate grinned at the mention of a plow horse. "You takin' up plowin' are you? You and that loose-jointed kid gonna be sodbusters are you? Hank'll shore be pleased to hear that you two are farmin'. So will Shorty. He ain't smiled since you busted two of his jaw teeth." Agate started squinting as the grin shaped into a smirk. In the half light of the shop's interior, his one eye looked like a cracked marble.

Kenyon spoke. "Listen, Agate, whatever I do or don't do in this town is my business."

Agate's smirk disappeared as hatred took its place. "Not for long it won't be, drifter. Not when I tell

Hank and Shorty. Shorty owes you, and he's just dyin' to pay his dues."

Herman led the team and wagon out to the street.

Agate leaped aboard and took the reins. "Put it on Mr. Terrell's bill . . . and you might do the undertaker a favor, and tell him to build a couple more pine boxes." He glanced at Kenyon. "I think he'll be needin' 'em." He grinned once more at Kenyon and cackled as he drove away.

"That von . . . he's a strange man," Herman said with a shake of his head. "Coo coo, that's vat he is. That eye . . . it gives me creeps."

"Yeah," Kenyon added, "he's a real prize. Now let's look at that horse."

It was a sturdy animal, broad in the chest and thick in the legs, and it stood nearly eighteen hands high.

"I tink maybe he's part Percheron. That's good verk horse ve have in Old Country," Herman commented.

"You got a reasonable wagon to go along with it?" Kenyon asked.

Herman beamed. "Ya! I fix you up good!"

It was nearly dusk by the time Kenyon returned, driving the wagon with his horse tied on behind.

Helen came out to greet him. "Now that's what I call a real fine lookin' workhorse. Where'd you get that beauty? He looks kind of familiar."

"Herman the blacksmith sold him to me," Kenyon answered. "He said the animal and wagon were left to pay funeral expenses and square things with the storekeeper."

"Whose funeral expenses?" she inquired.

"I don't know . . . some farmer's that lived west of town."

Helen's eyes narrowed in anger. "I'll bet you anything Terrell's bunch had a hand in this. I think I knowed that feller they killed. Didn't know his name, but I seen him at the store several times buyin' supplies. He had a nice young wife and three tow-headed younguns.''

"Maybe he wasn't killed. He might of just got sick or somethin'. Could have been he just upped and died," Riley commented as he joined the discussion.

Helen cocked her head to one side and stared at Riley in amazement. "I think this boy's been in the sun too long, Kenyon."

Riley glanced quickly at Kenyon and caught the makings of a smile. He then looked down at the dirt and kicked half-heartedly at a small clod. "Could've been somethin' else . . . maybe . . . but it prob'ly wasn't. It was prob'ly that stinkin' Terrell and his Circle T bunch. That's prob'ly who it was."

Helen winked at Kenyon. "You know this boy's gettin' to be a real judge of people." Her voice took on a serious note.

Riley looked up and saw Helen smiling at him. It was a warm smile, not a poking-fun-at-you smirk. He grinned. "You think so?"

"Sure she does," Kenyon said. "Now unsaddle my horse and put him in the corral while I unhitch this wagon. It'll be dark in a minute."

In the days that followed, Kenyon and Riley completed the room on the side of the cow shed. It had a window on one end and a door in the center. Kenyon covered the window with coyote skin that had the hair removed. The skin had been scraped clean, and when it was oiled and stretched taut over the window frame; it let in light but kept out the wind. The room was large enough to accommodate the two beds that Kenyon planned on building. Of course, in the wintertime when the cow spent its nights next door, it might be a little difficult to sleep, for cows are not known to be housebroken.

It was during the third night in their new quarters

that Kenyon was awakened by a loud voice calling in the dark.

"Hey, Miz Tilsbury, I just thought me and the boys would stop by and say hello, seein' as to how you're such a nice friendly lady," Hank's voice called.

"Maybe she's got some coffee to offer us, Hank." Shorty's voice was unmistakable.

The two of them laughed at the thought of Helen inviting them in.

"Hey, how about some coffee, Miz Tilsbury. We've come a long way just to see you," Hank said.

"What's goin' on?" Riley asked, sitting up.

"Shh!" Kenyon said. "It's Hank and Shorty and the boys comin' to cause trouble again."

"I wouldn't give you a glass of panther pee if you was dyin' of thirst," Helen replied, and with that she fired a shot through the window and nicked one of Terrell's men in the fleshy part of his upper arm. "Now get off my land 'fore I put a hole through one of you."

"Let's drag the old bitch out!" Shorty said.

"You go one step closer, Shorty, and I'll put a bullet right between those ears of yours and let that swamp water you got for brains run out on the ground." Kenyon's voice was loud and clear. "Now, Hank, you and that little prairie-dog pecker and the rest of you back-shooters get the hell out of here. Now!" Kenyon fired a shot and blew Hank's hat off his head.

Everyone left in a hurry. When they were away from the house, they stopped and Hank called back. "Is that you, Kenyon? I wondered where you was hidin'. Well, you'd better stay hidden 'cause the next time I see you, I'm gonna kill you!"

Kenyon fired one more shot in the general direction and heard a yell as someone took a flesh wound.

Hank's men fired several shots in return and then rode off. The slugs missed the house and landed harmlessly in the field beyond.

"You okay, Miz Tilsbury?" Riley asked.

"I'm fine, son, just fine thanks to you boys. You get some sleep now, and I'll see you in the mornin'."

"Yes, ma'am," he answered. Then, lowering his voice, he asked Kenyon, "Do you think they'll come back?"

"Not tonight," Kenyon said. "We took the wind out of their sails."

"What are we gonna do about goin' into town for supplies now?" Riley asked, with worry creeping into his voice.

"We'll go in like we always have," Kenyon said.

"What about Hank? He said he'd kill you next time he saw you."

"Hell, kid, if I stopped and worried every time somebody threatened me, I'd have died a bundle of nerves years ago. Now let's get some shut-eye. I'm tired."

9

KENYON LAY HALF-AWAKE ENJOYING THE luxury of sleeping on a bed, one of the two that he and Riley had made the day before. They were sturdy affairs made of log frames with leather-strap webbing forming the bottoms of the beds. Canvas tarps stuffed with hay and hand-stitched along their borders formed the mattresses. They might have been considered rough and ungainly in some quarters, but to Kenyon and Riley they were pure heaven. Kenyon's eyelids were beginning to flutter as he dozed again when Helen's voice rang out in the clear morning air.

"Come git this breakfast 'fore I throw it to the hogs."

Kenyon smiled as he opened his eyes. Helen didn't own any hogs. That was her way of calling them in to eat.

"Come on, Riley, shake a leg. Breakfast is ready," he said.

When they walked into the cabin, he and the Kid were both surprised to see Helen dressed in her best outfit.

"If I'd known you were going to dress up just to serve breakfast, I'd have worn a coat and tie," Kenyon said.

Helen snorted. "My guess is you ain't got a coat and tie, and if you did, you wouldn't wear 'em." Removing her apron she continued, "After breakfast I want you to drive me into town today in the wagon. I'm meetin' the other ladies in church. After the services, we're gonna take up a collection from among ourselves so we can buy some bobbed wire, and run a fence around the outside of the whole shebang. Then you and Riley can start earnin' your keep."

Kenyon looked up from his meal and did some mental calculating. "Since there are eight of you and you each own a quarter section, that's two full sections. And if they're in square sections, that means one hell of a lot of wire just to put up a one-strand fence."

"You got any better ideas to keep Terrell's cattle off our land and away from the crops we're gonna plant?" she asked.

"Maybe we can get the circuit judge to make Terrell pay for a fence, or at least pay for half of one since his property is on the other side."

"Kenyon, you sound like you left your head out yonder in the cow pen this mornin'. Terrell's a powerful man in these parts. He ain't about to pay fer nothin' he don't want to pay fer. Anyhow, we'll go ahead and buy the wire, and if you want to talk to the circuit judge when he comes into town, that's your business. Now finish your breakfast."

"Have you gotten an answer on your telegram to the marshal yet?"

"No," she answered, "nary a word."

"I should have ridden into Phoenix and delivered it to him in person," Kenyon said.

"Just take it easy. He'll send word directly."

The ride into town was quieter than usual. Riley was sitting on the end of the wagon bed with the tailgate down. Helen sat next to Kenyon as he drove the team. Finally Riley could keep still no longer. He got up and crouched down right behind the seat so he could talk and be heard.

"If Kenyon and I are usin' this horse and wagon to

haul fence posts and wire, what are you gonna use to go back and forth to town in?"

Helen glanced over her shoulder at him. "That's no problem, Riley. It just so happens that Alpha bought a horse and buggy of her own."

Kenyon stopped the wagon in front of the church and helped Helen down.

"Why don't you talk to some of those farmers again and see if you can convince them to join us?" he asked.

"I've talked to them men and their families till I'm blue in the face, and they still ain't decided," she sighed. "But I'll try again."

"Well, maybe the Holy Spirit will get in their bones this time. While you're listenin' to all that preachin', I'll see if I can find a good plow for you. I'll be back in about an hour."

"Maybe you two ought to come in with me. A little of God's word never hurt nobody." She looked at them expectantly.

Kenyon grinned. "I think me and the Almighty get along just fine. Besides, I've got work to do. Now maybe Riley here would like—"

"I . . . I've got to help Kenyon. Yessir! We've got to find a good plow, and since he ain't a farmer, it stands to reason he won't know nothin' about the fine points to look for in a first-rate plow."

Helen smiled. "I'll see you back here in an hour if God ain't struck you down by then."

After she walked away, Kenyon headed the wagon for Herman Konig's blacksmith shop. When they arrived, Herman was not to be found. A stable hand from the livery next door told them that Herman always attended church on Sundays.

Kenyon looked around the shop and found a plow that needed repairing. He made a mental note to ask Herman about it.

"Let's go over to the store, Kid, and see if Mr. Brownlee's got some barbed wire in stock."

They left the wagon and walked. Riley was quiet and very nervous as they rounded the corner and went down the main street. He kept looking from one side of the street to the other, and every fifth or sixth step he'd glance back over his shoulder to check the street behind them.

"What in the world's eatin' you, Riley? You act like the devil himself is on your tail this mornin'."

"Don't you 'member what Hank said? About killin' you next time he saw you?"

Kenyon grinned. "With a champion worrier like you for a pardner, why should I let it bother me?"

"Well, dang it, Kenyon, he might just step out of one of these buildin's along here and shoot you full of holes. That's enough to make anybody worry."

Kenyon laughed and gave Riley's shoulder a friendly slap. "This is Sunday mornin', Kid. Hank probably got drunk last night, and he won't be fit for man nor beast to be around 'til this afternoon sometime. But, thanks for bein' concerned." His face grew serious. "I mean that, Kid. I ain't had anybody worry about me for a coon's age."

Mr. Brownlee was standing just outside the door of his general store as they walked up. He was a thin little man with a pinched face, and he wore glasses with wire frames. His bald head had a fringe of hair running around the base from one sideburn to the other, and with his back toward them, as he was now standing, Mr. Brownlee's head reminded Kenyon of a bird's nest.

"Mornin'!" Kenyon said.

Mr. Brownlee jumped a little. Turning quickly, he gave a sickly smile in an attempt to cover his startled expression.

"Good morning," he managed.

"You got any barbed wire in this store of yours?"

"I do," he answered, "but it isn't for sale."

Kenyon frowned.

"Why?"

Mr. Brownlee cleared his throat and swallowed dryly. "It belongs to Mr. Terrell."

"How much is his?"

"All I've got stored in the backroom, plus a couple of railroad cars full of it down on the siding."

"It'll take him a month of Sundays to get it all made into fences. So why don't you sell me some, and you can put back what we take when a new shipment comes in."

"I can't do that. Mr. Terrell has spoken for that wire, and when he's ready to use it, whenever that may be, he'll have it waiting for him."

"So he hasn't actually bought the wire yet. Is that it?"

"That's correct, but Mr. Terrell often orders supplies and then pays for them at the end of the month."

"I see," Kenyon replied. "Let's go, Kid."

"What are we gonna do about the wire?" Riley asked, as they headed down the street.

"If Helen has the money together, we'll buy the wire and load it on the wagon."

"But Mr. Brownlee said—"

"I think Mr. Brownlee will be changin' his mind," Kenyon cut in. "He kind of seems like the type."

Riley studied Kenyon's face, wondering what he'd missed in the discussion back at the store. He soon gave it up, however, figuring time would tell him soon enough.

The broken plow in Herman Konig's blacksmith shop had been left by the same family that had left the horse and wagon Kenyon had purchased earlier. Herman said he'd fix the plow and have it ready within the hour. Kenyon left Riley at the shop and went back to the church to meet Helen.

Helen was standing to the left of the church's entrance surrounded by the widows who'd homesteaded land. They were having a discussion as Kenyon walked up. Helen, seeing him arrive, directed her next question at him.

"Alpha here tells me that there's bobbed wire at the store, but old Brownlee won't sell it to us. Says it all belongs to Terrell."

"That's right," Kenyon said nodding.

"Well, what are we gonna do for a fence?" Helen asked.

"Have you got the money for the wire?"

She cocked her head in bewilderment.

"Well . . . yeah, but you just said Brownlee wouldn't sell it to us."

"Brownlee has the wire, but Terrell has laid claim to it. I figure that since Terrell hasn't paid for it yet, it ain't really his. He has two railroad cars full of it down at the siding anyhow. It'll take him six months to put all of that into fencing."

"That is, if he was in a hurry to fence off his spread, which he ain't," Helen said. "All that lizard wants to do is keep us from gettin' it."

Kenyon grinned. "That's what I figured too. Now I'll need more than just one wagon to haul it in."

Alpha spoke. "You can use mine."

Two other women added, "We'll rent a couple wagons at the livery stable. Will that be enough?"

"I think that'll do just fine. If you ladies will just follow me, we'll buy ourselves a fence."

When they arrived at Herman's shop, Helen paid him for the plow, and he set it up in the back of her wagon. Her two friends went next door to rent the wagons. Then she told Riley, "You drive this down to Brownlee's store. We're buyin' some wire."

"Take the wagon around to the back, Riley," Kenyon added, "and, Helen, tell your friends over at the livery to do the same. I'm going to have a little talk with Mr. Brownlee."

"You hang on a minute, Kenyon, 'cause I'm goin' with you," Helen said.

As they passed the livery stable, Helen told her friends where to drive the wagons; then, she and Kenyon headed for Brownlee's General Store.

Mr. Brownlee looked up over the top of his glasses as Helen and Kenyon entered. Then, turning on the charm, he stepped out from behind the counter smiling broadly. "Good morning to you, Mrs. Tilsbury. And what can I do for you today?"

"I've got four wagons comin' up to your back door. I want 'em filled with rolls of bobbed wire."

Still trying to appear jovial, Brownlee had to work at keeping his smile. "I'm afraid that just isn't possible. You see Mr. Terrell has—"

"Not paid for the wire," Kenyon interrupted, "so there's nothin' wrong with our buyin' it."

"Mr. Terrell spoke for that wire and—"

"Speakin' fer it and payin' fer it are two different things," Helen added. "Ben Terrell has two box cars loaded with wire. Now the only reason he 'spoke' fer them rolls you've got in your back room is because we need it, and what's more, Mr. Brownlee, we aim to take it."

"Now hold on. Taking property that doesn't belong to you is robbery."

"Then Terrell's the biggest thief around," Kenyon said. "He's been takin' land that doesn't belong to him by killin' off the owners. Besides, we're payin' for the wire, not stealin' it." He took the money Helen handed him and stuffed in inside Brownlee's shirt. "Now you take that and count it, and then write us out a sales receipt."

"Mr. Terrell's not going to like this," Brownlee said, counting the bills.

"We never figured he would," Kenyon said. "Now get that back door open so we can load up."

Brownlee reluctantly opened the back door and was greeted by three women and a grinning Riley, waiting with four wagons.

"There's going to be trouble about this, and you can bet on it!" Brownlee exclaimed.

"Trouble ain't no stranger to this crowd," Helen commented. "Alright, let's git them wagons loaded 'fore Mr. Brownlee here has a kitten."

Brownlee gave Helen a sour look and marched back inside his store. Within a few minutes his storeroom was cleaned out, and the wagons were on their way. Brownlee took off his apron, put on his coat, locked his door, and headed for the livery stable to hire himself a horse and buckboard.

10

AFTER THE WAGONS WERE UNLOADED, HELEN invited everyone to have some coffee and cake. When the socializing was finished, she walked Alpha back out to her wagon and spoke to her quietly. Then they smiled at each other, and Alpha drove off accompanied by Lydia Nofzigger and Alice Bruckerman, each driving her own wagon.

"They're gonna bring them wagons back tomorrow, and you can drive to them mountains yonder and cut a load of fence posts."

"Sounds good," Kenyon said. "The more hands we have cuttin', the faster it'll go." Turning to Riley he said, "Come on, Kid, let's start clearin' some ground so you can show Miz Tilsbury here how well you can handle that plow."

It was nearly two hours later when they stopped to take a breather that Riley saw the riders coming over the ridge in back of Helen's cabin.

"Looks like the Circle T bunch, and they're ridin' hard."

Kenyon rose and looked. "Yeah, that's who it is, and Terrell's right out in front. You hightail it to our shack, Kid, and get my rifle, but watch 'em through the window. Don't come outside."

Terrell yanked the reins so hard that his big roan reared up on its hind legs and whinnied loudly.

"Mistreatin' a horse ain't gonna git you nothin' but

my contempt, Ben Terrell," Helen said, stepping out with her rifle cocked and ready.

"I came to get my wire."

"Your wire is in two boxcars on the siding in town," Kenyon said, as he walked into Helen's front yard. "Far as I know, it's still there."

Ben Terrell glanced at his foreman. "Hank!"

On that word, four of the six men that accompanied Terrell trained their guns on Kenyon. Hank was one of them, and he nudged his horse forward a few steps to separate himself from the group.

"I don't believe Mr. Terrell was talkin' to you, saddle tramp. So I think I'd keep my mouth shut if I was you." Then to show his contempt for Kenyon, he holstered his gun.

"I didn't know you could think, Hank," Kenyon replied quietly.

Hank's jaw muscles twitched in anger, but it was obvious to Kenyon that the man was under orders from Terrell not to start anything until he was given the word.

That was an advantage to Kenyon, for as long as a man is under orders not to shoot until told, he's a sitting duck.

Terrell continued. "Mr. Brownlee said you forced him to sell my wire to you."

"Mr. Brownlee didn't tell the truth. He sold us wire that nobody owned. You hadn't paid for it, so it wasn't yours," Kenyon said.

Hank kicked his buckskin, and it leaped forward.

Kenyon stepped lightly aside and the buckskin just missed his shoulder. Reaching up, he caught Hank by the belt and yanked him from the saddle. With the buckskin between Kenyon and Terrell's three gun hands, they couldn't shoot for fear of hitting either Hank or his horse. Hank fell heavily to the ground stunning him momentarily. Kenyon used his opportunity and grabbed Hank by the front of his shirt, making him struggle to his feet. By the time the buckskin had moved to one side, Kenyon had a gun pointed at Hank's head.

"Tell your friends to drop their irons."

Hank waved his hand at them. "Do what he says, boys."

The three men glanced at Terrell, who nodded at them to do as Hank requested. They dropped their guns reluctantly.

"Now back up a half a dozen steps," Kenyon ordered. When they complied, he pulled Hank's gun from its holster and gave him a hard shove at the same time. "You join 'em over there, gordo."

As Hank stumbled forward, Kenyon bent down to pick up the guns. One of the other two cowhands who'd been near Terrell's side slowly reached for his weapon.

Alpha's voice rang loud and clear from the rocks near Helen's cabin.

"I wouldn't touch that gun of yours if I was you, Buster. You might lose a hand."

The cowboy's hand stopped, and everyone looked toward the rocks. They couldn't see anyone. They looked back at Terrell for guidance.

"You got women doing your fighting for you now, Kenyon?"

Kenyon grinned. "A whole regiment of 'em, and they're a damned sight better than these sad cases you've got on your payroll."

"That's one more I owe you, drifter," Hank said. "It'll be payday one of these days, and that's when you're gonna be cashin' in."

Kenyon ignored Hank and didn't even bother to acknowledge the threat. "Terrell," he said, "I think it's time for you and your back-shooters to get out of here. You only wanted that wire to keep us from gettin' it. Well, it didn't work, so ride out and let well enough alone."

"If you think a few strands of wire is going to keep my herd from using this land, you're crazy. This land belongs to me, and I aim to take it. If not today, then tomorrow is fine, or the next day, or the next."

"I'll shoot every one of the danged longhorns that comes onto my property," Helen said.

"You do and I'll make you wish you'd never seen the Arizona Territory."

"Get the hell out of here, Terrell, and take this buzzard bait with you," Kenyon said. "I don't abide women being threatened."

Terrell spun the big roan into a half circle and rode out followed by his ranch hands.

After they'd gone, Alpha and Lydia came out from behind the big boulders.

Kenyon glanced at Helen and raised one eyebrow. "So that's what you two were whisperin' about just before the wagons left."

Helen smiled. "I figured that sidewinder would come a-callin' just as soon as old Brownlee could make it out to the Circle T to spill the beans about the wire. I figured we could use an extra gun or two."

"Make that three," Riley said, stepping out of the shack still carrying Kenyon's rifle. "Boy I had my sights trained on that fella, and I'd have cut him in two, if he'd gone for his gun."

"Action like this is apt to make a man real hungry," Helen said with mock seriousness. "I'll bet you're half-starved right now, ain't you?"

"Well, yes ma'am I could do with a bite or two," he answered.

"Or ten or twelve," Kenyon commented.

Kenyon, Riley, and four women spent the next few days in the hills cutting wood for fence posts. When they'd filled four wagons, they left.

Helen was glad to see them return.

"That no account Terrell had his boys drive a couple

of hundred head of longhorns through here yesterday. They stomped my garden right into the soil again. Nary a thing left but some tracks."

"We'll get some wire strung tomorrow and maybe that'll slow 'em down some," Riley said.

"Have you gotten any word on that telegram yet?" Kenyon asked.

"Nope. I'm beginnin' to wonder if that marshal ain't cut from the same cloth as Ed Wallace."

"I'll take a ride into town and do some checkin'. That's too long a time. We should have heard somethin' by now."

"Well, let's wait til we git some wire strung up. That's more important to me right now than the law."

"What about the other homesteaders? Are any of 'em gonna join you and the other women?" Kenyon asked.

"They're all afraid to even come to a meetin', let alone join us to fight against Terrell. I called two different meetin's and nobody even bothered to show up. I wouldn't give you a plug nickel fer the whole bunch of 'em. I know they got younguns to worry about, but shoot . . . they ought to show some backbone."

Ben Terrell sat holding a large glass of whiskey as he gazed at the map on the wall of his living room. Hank, holding a smaller glass, sat next to him and stared at the same map. Terrell had outlined, in red, the farms he'd brought the women out to homestead for him. They formed a patchwork of twelve quarter-sections, three square miles of land. Four of the twelve had an *X* drawn through the center of each. The other eight formed a crescent that separated the Circle T Ranch from government-owned open range, and there were no *X*'s on them.

"Them goddamn women have got to go, Hank. If they don't, sooner or later they'll have the law on their side, and I won't be able to graze my herd on that open range. There ain't no other way to get to it except over the top of that damned mountain, and I ain't doin' that."

"Old lady Tilsbury's the one that's got 'em all churned up," Hank said. "She's crappin' in tall cotton now that she's got that drifter Kenyon backin' her up. I think if we shoot that sonofabitch, it'll take the wind right out of her sails. She couldn't do doodly squat without him as her ace in the hole."

Terrell took a large gulp from his glass and then bit the tip off of a long black cigar, spitting the piece into the huge rock fireplace to his left. "I don't want no killin' around them old ladies if we can help it. They'll squawk loud enough to raise the dead if he gets himself shot on their doorstep."

"It don't have to be around where they can see it," Hank said. "Either Kenyon or that skinny-ass kid does the shoppin' for old lady Tilsbury. Alls we have to do is shoot one of 'em on the way in."

Terrell looked quizzically at Hank for a moment. "Speakin' of that kid Riley, where was he when we rode out there? You think he might have taken off on his own?"

"No, he'd starve to death without somebody leadin' him to the trough. Hey, I just had me an idea! Why don't we grab the kid, and then we can make Kenyon do whatever we want. We tell him to ride out, or we fill the kid full of lead."

Terrell grinned and raised his glass in a toast to Hank's brilliant suggestion. "Maybe the whole thing can be taken care of without firing a shot. Hank, you did yourself proud with that idea."

Hank beamed with pride and swallowed the rest of the whiskey in his glass, so he could take advantage of the refill Terrell was offering. "I'll take care of it right away, Mr. Terrell."

When Hank left the main house, he felt like he was walking on a cloud. It made a man feel great to be thought of so highly by his boss. Terrell had even given him the bottle of whiskey they had been drinking from.

Shorty was sitting in a chair that was tipped back against the bunkhouse as Hank walked up. His jaw still had a dull ache where Kenyon had broken those teeth. Doc Weaver had pulled them out the day after the fight, but he had torn up Shorty's gums pretty badly while he was doing it. He had put a poultice of boiled and crushed herbs on the gum and then bound Shorty's mouth shut with a bandage that went underneath the jaw and over the top of his head several times. Shorty had eaten no solid food in the week that followed. Now, even a couple of weeks after the bandage was removed, he still had a tough time eating. Soup drawn up through a hollow reed didn't qualify as a meal in Shorty's opinion. The pain had persisted every day since the fight, and he hated Kenyon for it. He looked sourly at Hank, for he knew the big man had seldom been hurt in a fight. Now he'd just come from the main house with a bottle in his hand and the smell of liquor on his breath. Hank's grin irritated him.

"What in the hell are you grinnin' about?" he grumbled.

"I've got some good news for you, Shorty. We're gonna grab that Riley kid the next time he goes into town."

Shorty stared at Hank and tried to get the full impact of what he'd just been told, but his expression showed bewilderment.

"Don't you get it? If we grab the kid, we can make Kenyon do anything we want. We can run him out of the country."

"I want to kill him," Shorty mumbled.

"I reckon we can do that too, pardner. Come on in and I'll pour you a drink."

Shorty's face broke into a happy smile, the first he'd had in nearly a month.

* * *

Kenyon and Riley had strung a lot of wire in the days that had passed since Terrell's longhorns had ruined Helen's garden, but the fence didn't stretch very far. Each day when they drove the wagon out to start work again, they'd find large sections of the fence torn down, and would have to rebuild.

"If this keeps up, we're never gonna finish this fence." Riley said.

"You're right," Kenyon observed. "So we're goin' to stand guard. Anybody that cuts this wire tonight gets some lead in return. If we don't let them know we mean business, they'll push us off the land."

"We gonna stay up all night?"

"I don't think we'll have to," Kenyon answered. "I figure they'll come before midnight. They have to get up early in the mornin' to work too you know."

Riley stood the first watch. He rode out to the area where the Circle T had done the most wire cutting and tethered his horse among some boulders on a slight knoll where he'd have a clear view of several hundred yards of fence in both directions.

It was after ten o'clock when Kenyon showed up.

"Seen anything, Kid?"

"Not yet. You reckon they'll come tonight?"

"I imagine. With all the fun they're havin' tearin' down our fence, you can bet they'll be back tonight."

"Good!" Riley commented. "I wouldn't mind puttin' a couple of slugs into that fat-ass Hank."

Kenyon grinned. "You sound downright bloodthirsty, Kid."

"Well that just fries my hide that he'd come around pickin' on Miz Tilsbury. You'd think that—"

Kenyon motioned for Riley to stop talking as he peered over the boulder. Three Circle T riders were coming down the side of a hill about two hundred yards on the other side of the fence.

"I'll head for that rock over there," Kenyon said, pointing to a boulder about fifty yards away. "Wait 'til I get there before you do anything."

"I'll let you fire first," Riley said.

"We don't want to kill 'em, just wound 'em a little," Kenyon cautioned; then, he took off in a crouching run and made it to the rocks just as the three horsemen reached the fence.

Kenyon eased his Winchester over the top of the rock and took aim at one of the cowboys who had dismounted and was about to cut the wire near a fence post about twenty yards from Kenyon's rock. The other two were forming loops with their lariats so they could rope some fence posts and pull them out of the ground.

Kenyon motioned to Riley to shot the wire cutter, and he'd shoot at the two ropers. The instant he had one of the roper's shoulders in his sights, he squeezed the trigger. The cowboy let out a yell and dropped his lariat. An instant later Riley's shot hit the wire cutter in the hand, causing him to drop the cutters and yell out in pain.

The third rider drew his pistol and fired two shots at the rocks, then took off at a gallop. The one Kenyon hit reeled in the saddle like a drunk as he turned his horse and headed toward the Circle T.

The first man, his arm hanging loosely at his side, mounted his horse and took off at a dead run for the Circle T.

Riley came out from behind the rocks grinning. "I guess we taught them a thing or two."

"Yeah," Kenyon answered, "it was a good night's work. We hit two of them, and we got ourselves a rope and a pair of wire cutters they left behind. We also bought ourselves a peck of trouble when Ben Terrell makes his next move."

11

Hank was awakened as the first of the three riders came into the yard at a dead run. He slipped on his boots and stepped outside. Jason was tying his horse to the hitching rail as Hank walked up.

"They shot the hell out of us," Jason said. "They hit Griggs, and I think they hit Agate."

"You think!" Hank thundered.

Jason countered angrily. "They was hid behind some rocks, and we couldn't see anything to shoot at. When they hit the other two, I lit out. It was like shootin' fish in a barrel to them. I wasn't about to stay there and get blown out of the saddle."

The two of them turned as one at the sound of two horses coming into the yard.

Terrell stepped out wearing only a pair of pants. "What's goin' on, Hank?"

"Griggs and Agate got shot up over at old lady Tilsbury's fence. Must have been Kenyon and that kid."

"Well, hitch up the buckboard and take 'em both in to see Doc Weaver. We'll settle old Tilsbury's hash tomorrow. It feels like it might rain, and I ain't about to ride out in wet weather just to take care of that old biddy." He went back into the house.

After Doc Weaver had patched up Griggs and Agate and grabbed the last two hours of darkness for some much needed sleep, he had breakfast and walked over to the sheriff's office to have a talk with Ed Wallace.

Ed was just pouring himself a cup of coffee as Doc entered.

"Mornin', Doc. You want a cup of coffee?"

"No, thanks. I've tried that embalming fluid you call coffee before. It ruined my digestion for a week."

"What can I do for you?"

"I want to talk to you about what's happening outside of town. You know, that area you never travel in."

"Now what in the hell's that supposed to mean?" Ed growled.

"You know exactly what I mean," Doc replied. "I just patched up two of Terrell's men for gunshot wounds. Now you know they didn't shoot each other."

"So what do you want me to do? I don't know anything about it."

"You don't know because you don't *want* to know," Doc said. "In the last year I've doctored quite a few people with gunshot wounds. Some of them died and some didn't, but I haven't seen you bring one man into this jail for doing the shooting. What does it take to get you off your ass, a full-scale war?"

"Now just a damned minute here, Doc. I don't come into your office and try to tell you how to take care of your patients, so you just keep your nose out of the law business."

"You don't know the first thing about law and justice, Ed. You only enforce the kind of law that Ben Terrell believes in. You know what he's been doing out there. He's trying to push that widow off her land. Now those two men I patched up last night sure as hell didn't get those bullets holes from playing mumble peg. She's trying to defend her land, and if you don't do something about helping her, there's going to be a lot more bloodshed. Some of it may be hers. How would you feel to know that she was gunned down because you were too damned chicken to uphold the law?"

"You've got one hell of a big mouth, Doc. You're talkin' about somethin' you don't know nothin' about. In the first place, Mr. Terrell paid those widows to come out here and homestead the land for him. Now that old lady is sayin' that she ain't gonna turn the land over to Mr. Terrell. She's gonna keep it for herself, and she's tryin' to turn all the others against Mr. Terrell too."

"Ain't it illegal to homestead land for somebody else?" Doc asked.

"Not if they homestead it and then decide to sell it later, it ain't."

"Well, it's sure as hell illegal to try and run somebody off her land if she's set on keeping it for herself and it's legally hers."

"Doc, this conversation is at an end. Get the hell out of here. I don't need you to start off my day with a ration of crap."

Doc left the sheriff's office mumbling about gutless wonders.

Ben Terrell was up at the rooster's crow. He took a steak from the platter of cooked meat destined for the hired hands and began chewing on it. It was good beef. Of course he had the best grass land around, and the government range could be reached only by going over his land. At least it would be his just as soon as he drove those trouble-making women off of it.

They had their nerve. When the government had allowed widows of soldiers killed in the war to homestead a quarter section—160 acres—no one was taking the government up on its offer until he had made the generous announcement that he'd pay them one hundred dollars plus train fare to homestead the land and then turn it over to him. Now there were eight of them who had backed out on the deal, wanted the land for themselves. Well, he thought, they ain't stoppin' my herd from that open range. I'll drive over the top of them if I have to.

He finished his steak and coffee and then stepped outside to check the weather. It had started to cloud up and could easily bring rain by midday or late afternoon. As soon as the boys finished eating, he'd tell Hank what to do.

Helen waited until Kenyon and Riley were seated at the table and she'd served up platters of sourdough pancakes and over-easy eggs before she spoke. "How'd things go last night? I thought I heard some shootin', but I wasn't sure. Did Terrell's bunch cut any of our fence?"

Riley grinned. "They tried, but we shot a couple of 'em, and they hightailed out."

Helen's eyes narrowed with concern. "You didn't . . . kill anybody, did you?"

Kenyon started to speak, but Riley was enjoying the recounting of last night's shoot-out so much, he decided to let the Kid bask in the glory of his first gunfight.

"Naw, we didn't kill nobody. We knew what we was doin'. We just winged 'em good and proper. I shore don't thank they'll be a-cuttin' wire fer quite a spell."

"Sounds right to me," Kenyon added. "A man doesn't like to ride into something he can't see. Now that they know we mean business, they'll try somethin' else."

"What you reckon they'll do . . . blast us out?" she asked.

"No, I think Terrell will probably have his boys run his herd through here."

"He tried that before, and all they did was tramp down my garden."

"You haven't begun to see the herd Terrell has. All he did was run a hundred or so through here. Wait till the boys drive a thousand of 'em through. It'll make this place look like a new-plowed field."

"The two men that built this house told me they had heard of adobe buildin's with saguaro-rib roofs that have withstood the force of stampedin' cattle runnin' squarely across the top of the danged things," Helen said.

"I've heard that too," Kenyon said, "but I wouldn't want to test it out. Besides, those kinds of houses are built mostly into the side of a hill with the roof at ground level. That's quite different from what you've got here."

"Then, what can we do about it?" she asked.

"Well," Kenyon said thinking over the problem, "trying to change direction of a herd that size is pretty dangerous, especially if they're movin' right along." Then his face lit up as he thought of something that might work. "It might be possible to make the herd go in a dozen different directions at once. If we can do that, it'll drive some of them right back on top of Terrell's bunch and scatter the rest of those cows from here to Timbucktu. When they finally do stop runnin', they'll have lost a good fifty pounds apiece, and it'll keep Terrell's whole crew busy for a month just tryin' to get them back on his range."

Riley was all smiles. "How do we do it?"

"I noticed there was a storage shed near those two railroad cars that Terrell has all of his wire in. They often use dynamite when they have to build spur lines and such. If they've got any in the shed, we'll just borrow some of it. I haven't seen an animal yet that won't get spooked when a stick of dynamite goes off nearby."

"That's a great idea. You want me to saddle the horses?"

"Not yet. The weather's going to help us with some black clouds and heavier rain before night falls. It'll be hard for any of Terrell's crew to see us after it gets a little darker, and since you and I were responsible for shooting up two of Terrell's men, it wouldn't be too healthy a situation for either of us to be caught in town by any of the Circle T bunch."

By the time dusk had settled, the afternoon rain had become a steady drizzle. Kenyon and the Kid took off for town. They rode east for about a mile and then cut south to avoid the main road. By the time they reached town, it was very dark. The moon was in the first phase of a new quarter, and heavy black clouds were obscuring the thin crescent of light that fought its way over the junipered ridge to the north.

For safety purposes the storage shed used by the railroad was a good quarter of a mile from the station house. Kenyon and Riley tied their mounts behind the shed so that the stationmaster, should he look in their direction, would see nothing suspicious. With the steady rain and the heavy cloud cover, it was very unlikely that he could even see that far.

A low rumbling peal of thunder shot down the side of the distant mountains, gathered speed as it crossed the desert, and ended in a deafening crash almost directly overhead.

Kenyon examined the heavy lock that the company used for security. There was no way that it could be broken with a gun butt. He drew his Colt and held it ready. When the next bolt of lighting flashed to the north, he waited a few seconds and then fired into the lock so that the gunshot would coincide with the thunder clap that shook the area. The lock gave way, and he and Riley stepped inside the shed. He lit a match and glanced around the room. In one corner, three boxes of dynamite were stacked. In another corner were caps and fuses. He opened the small box of caps and shoved a handful in his pocket. Then, handing Riley a coiled length of fuse, he opened one of the boxes of dynamite and took out a dozen sticks. Tucking them under his rain slicker, he said, "Let's get out of here."

"Them sticks ain't gonna go off 'fore we get home, are they?"

Kenyon grinned. "Not unless I get hit by a streak of lightin'."

Riley lagged behind for the rest of the trip. They took the main road now, confident that no one would be watching for them in the rain.

The steady drizzle changed as the wind gained strength. The whole sky seemed to open up, and the rain came down in great sheets. When the faint glow of the coal-oil lamp Helen had in her window broke through the wet darkness, both Kenyon and Riley breathed a sigh of relief.

Helen yelled that she had some hot coffee for them, and as soon as they had taken off the saddles and rubbed down their horses, they both made a beeline for the house.

"You don't reckon Terrell's bunch would be mean enough to come out and bother us on a night like this do you?" she asked as she filled their cups.

"Oh, they're mean enough, but no cowhand likes to be out in weather like this, and the best way for Terrell to lose some of them is to order them to ride out in a storm when tomorrow could do just as well. They won't be around till the storm lets up, and then . . . watch out!"

12

THE RAIN CONTINUED THROUGHOUT THE night and was still coming down hard when Kenyon and Riley went into Helen's kitchen for breakfast. By the time they had finished eating, however, the storm had passed over and was heading for New Mexico. Kenyon studied the patches of blue that had begun pushing their way boldly through the scattered cumulus clouds that rode drag on the storm.

"That's the last of the rain. I think we can expect the Circle T cattle to be coming through here pretty soon. Let's get the dynamite ready, Kid."

Kenyon took six of the sticks and put the caps in place, then stuck a five-minute fuse in each one. The remaining half-dozen sticks were fixed with short fifteen-second fuses. He then rode out and placed those with long fuses in a straight line across the downhill side of a natural saddle the cattle would have to cross coming onto Helen's homestead. He gave Riley two of the remaining sticks and kept four for himself. "Now," he said, "when the cattle hit the bottom of the little dip the other side of that saddle, I'll light all six of those dynamite fuses. By the time they cross the ridge of the saddle and start down this side, those sticks should go off. Then, you and I will ride behind the herd, throwing one of these short fuses into the stragglers in the rear every now and then just to keep them moving."

"How long do we stay with 'em?" Riley asked.

"Clear down to where that little box canyon comes in on the left side of the valley."

"That's a good four miles from here," Riley said.

Kenyon grinned. "More like five or six. If we can keep them running that far, I don't think Terrell's bunch will be giving us any trouble for at least a week or two. Well, are you ready?"

Riley beamed. "I sure am. I been waitin' fer somethin' like this fer quite a spell. Let's go!"

Hank and Shorty were riding point. Jason, Edgars, Miller, and Lang were on swing and flank, and four other Circle T hands were riding drag. Shorty crossed over in front of the herd and rode up next to Hank. "There ain't gonna be enough of old lady Tilsbury's place left to form a cross for a dead cat's grave."

Hank laughed. "I just hope Kenyon and that bag of bones pardner of his are around. I'd like to clean up this whole mess in one easy sweep."

Shorty chuckled. "I got a few paybacks to lay on both of them dudes." He rubbed his jaw. " 'Specially that Kenyon. If we see him, let me have the first shot. Okay, Hank?"

"Hell no! I owe him a few my own self. You're gonna have to outdraw me to get the first shot in."

Shorty laughed, revealing a noticeable gap where Kenyon's fist had taken its toll. "He'll think he was hit by a double-barrel shotgun when you and me both drill him at the same time." Then he laughed again and rode back to the other side of the herd.

Kenyon waited until the cattle had gone down the slope into the small meadow on the other side of the saddle before he ran out to light the five-minute fuses. Then he hurried back behind the rocks and mounted up. As he waited, he rolled and lit a cigarette so that he would have a ready source of heat to light the short fuses with. Within another couple of minutes, the herd drifted over the top of the saddle and started down the hill toward the rocky area where Kenyon and Riley were waiting.

Miller and Lang rode up from the flank position on the herd and passed Hank and Shorty as they headed for the fence to cut the wire. The cattle were crowding through the narrow seat of the saddle and spreading in a fan shape down the side of the hill toward the fence when the first charge went off. It was immediately followed by four more almost in unison, and then, after a few seconds delay, the sixth one exploded. There was instant panic in the herd. They turned in one bawling, shoving, wide-eyed, thundering mass and headed back in the direction they had come.

Miller and Lang were almost directly over the dynamite sticks when they exploded. They were thrown from their horses and trampled but not killed by the terror-striken cattle. Hank and Shorty were caught up in the center of the bawling cows and had to ride like the wind to keep from going under. Jason and Edgars were nowhere to be seen.

Kenyon and Riley raced out and caught up with the tail end of the herd yelling and firing their guns as they rode. Some of the cattle, caught between the bulk of the herd behind them and the crushing mass stampeding down the slope of the saddle in front of them, were trampled to death before they could spin around and join their panicked leaders.

When Kenyon and Riley reached an area where they could race along the side of the stampeding herd, they lit and threw the short-fused sticks as far as they could so they would explode in the center of the bellowing mass. The cattle responded by splitting the herd into two parts, each heading in a direction oblique to the one they had been running in and away from the terrible thundering noise that had blown sod into their faces.

When Kenyon had thrown the last of his sticks, he wheeled around and headed back to Helen's homestead. He met Riley on the way, and they had a good laugh.

"I don't think them cows will ever stop runnin'," Riley cackled. "If they do quit, there ain't gonna be nothin' left of 'em but a hank of hair and a pile of bones. There sure ain't gonna be no meat on 'em, that's fer danged sure."

"Maybe it will cause Terrell to think twice before he tries riding roughshod over the homesteaders again. *Maybe*," Kenyon emphasized the word, "but I doubt it."

"You mean you don't think he'll quit?" Riley asked.

"Would you?" Kenyon answered. "He won't rest until he's paid us back. You can bet on it."

When they reached the area of the first explosions, they saw Miller leaning against a rock with a broken leg and lots of cuts and bruises. If he'd had his gun still in its holster, he would have shot at them out of pure anger, but it was lost when he was pitched off his horse. Lang was still lying on the ground some distance away, unconscious.

Kenyon dismounted and rolled Lang over on his back. His cheekbone was crushed, and he had at least five broken ribs. He also had a deep gash made by a flying hoof right above his right eye, the probable cause of his unconsciousness.

"We'll bring the wagon around and take you boys into town to see Doc Weaver."

Miller looked at Kenyon with contempt. "I don't need help from the likes of you. You was the one that started them cattle to stampede in the first place."

"Go back and get the wagon, Riley."

"I said I didn't need no help. The Circle T boys will be back directly. They'll take care of me."

"I wouldn't bet cash money on it," Kenyon answered. "Cowhands like you are a dime a dozen to a man like Terrell. But those cattle . . . now that's a different story. They'll be busy for days tryin' to get all those Circle T cows back on the ranch. There won't be anyone comin' out here to see if you're okay, so you'd better take my offer while you can get it. As far as the stampede goes, of course it was me that started it. What would you have done if it was your place instead of Miz Tilsbury's? Let somebody drive a thousand head smack dab through the center of your house? You'd have done the same thing we did if you'd thought of it."

By the time Riley arrived with the wagon, Kenyon had made a splint of tree limbs for Miller's leg, and Lang was just coming to. Both men were helped into the back of the wagon, and then Riley drove them into town followed by Kenyon leading a Circle T horse with a bruised leg.

Doc Weaver greeted them with a scowl. "What the hell's going on back in those hills? We just had a couple of hundred cows running through here tearin' the hell out of everything."

"They got spooked," Riley said.

Doc stopped his bandaging and glared at Riley. "Now that's the most brilliant remark I've heard since Heck was a pup. Why in the hell else would they be runnin' hell-bent for election if they weren't spooked? The question is, what in the hell spooked them?"

"Gophers," Kenyon said.

"Gophers!" Doc exploded. Then a rumble started deep in his chest and erupted like a volcano as the laughter broke through to the surface. As Kenyon and Riley left the Doc's office, they heard him say the word *gophers* again and start another round of laughter, slapping Lang on the back as he did so. Lang let out a loud moan and began cursing Doc Weaver.

"Sounds like Lang's gonna make it," Riley said. Then he repeated the word *gophers* and broke out laughing.

13

As Kenyon predicted, the Circle T bunch was busy for two weeks rounding up Terrell's cattle and another week settling claims for damages pressed by smaller ranchers because of the destruction to their property caused by the wild-eyed steers carrying Circle T brands.

Terrell was fit to be tied. He had dwelled for three weeks on various methods of slow death he would like to thrust upon Kenyon and Riley. The stampede these two drifters had caused had run off a collective total of thousands of pounds of beef, meat that just disappeared, enough meat, Terrell figured, to feed the entire U.S. Cavalry west of the Mississippi. Kenyon and Riley were also responsible for putting four of Terrell's men out of commission for quite a while—Griggs and Agate with gunshot wounds, and Miller and Lang from being tromped on by several hundred scatterbrained, fear-crazed longhorns. Kenyon and Riley had a debt to pay, and by God they'd pay it one way or another. Terrell gave Hank and Shorty orders to go into town and stay in the rooms above the Buckboard, the saloon he owned, and not to return until they had Riley as a hostage or had killed Kenyon. Either way would bring a quick extraction of the giant thorn they had become in his side. With Kenyon dead, Riley would blow out of town like a dandelion gone to seed. If Riley were taken hostage, Kenyon would do as he was told to save

Riley's life. Both prospects of success brought a warm feeling inside Terrell's barrel chest.

Kenyon was surprised that he had no confrontation with Terrell's bunch in three weeks. He hadn't realized the full impact of the damage and destruction the longhorn locomotives of the Circle T had caused. He didn't know that some of them had run flat out for a ten-mile stretch in six different directions. So it was only natural that, being a curious man, he would want to ride into town with Helen and Riley to seek news about the results of his strategy.

While Helen was having her order filled at Brownlee's store, Kenyon sent Riley to do some quiet snooping around town to see what information he could dredge up about the Circle T. He himself decided to ride down to the telegraph office and check to see if the U.S. marshal had responded to Helen's telegram.

He dismounted and stepped inside the office. The clerk, a thin little man with an asthmatic wheeze that sounded like the dried-out packing on a water pump, looked up from under the green eyeshade he wore and said, "Paper and pencil's on the counter, and it's five cents a word. If you can't write, cool your heels for a minute, and I'll be right with you."

Kenyon decided he would send a message to the territorial governor and that, along with Helen's telegram to the U.S. marshal, should bring some quick response. He wrote the message and then counted out the money. The clerk was still busy reading a new edition of the *Atlantic Monthly*. Kenyon cleared his throat. "I'd like this sent before the new issue comes out."

The clerk reluctantly put the magazine down and walked to the counter, giving Kenyon a surly look all the while. As he read the message over for a word count, his eyes lit up at the mention of Terrell's name.

"Is that the right amount?" Kenyon asked.

"Ah . . . yes . . . yes, it is," the clerk answered without counting the money. "I'll send it off right away."

"Oh, by the way, Miz Tilsbury asked me to check on the telegram she sent to the U.S. marshal a while back. You did send it out, didn't you?" He leaned on the counter and looked the clerk directly in the eyes.

The little man licked his dry lips and tilted his head up and to the side so the stiff starched collar on his shirt wouldn't prevent him from swallowing. "Ah, yes . . . yes of course I sent it."

"I wonder why she hasn't gotten an answer yet?" Kenyon said, still staring at the clerk.

"I'm, ah . . . sure I don't know. Perhaps the marshal is busy with more important things. Now, if you'll excuse me, I'll send off that telegram to the marshal . . . ah . . . the governor."

"Yeah, you do that," Kenyon said, heading for the door.

The little asthmatic wheezer flitted about the office, taking off his green visor, plastering down the few wispy strands of hair that separated his ears from the broad expanse of naked skin that covered his head. He put on his coat. Then, he stepped out of his office, closed the door behind him, and skipped lightly around the corner where he ran into the barrel of Kenyon's Colt .45.

"I do declare that message you have in your hand there looks a great deal like the message I just wrote. Did you misplace your wireless?"

The clerk's face, already drawn and wrinkled, suddenly blanched of color and took on the appearance of a badly laundered sheet. "Ah . . . Ah. . ."

"You'd make a hell of a patient for a doctor," Kenyon said. "You've got the 'Ah' down pretty good. Maybe we ought to go back inside so you can send that message before you forget what you were hired for. What do you say?"

"Ah..."

"Good! Let's do," Kenyon said, turning the wheezer around.

After the clerk unlocked the office door, Kenyon followed him in and stood behind him until the message was sent. Then he spun the chair around and grabbed the clerk by his shoulder. "You didn't send Miz Tilsbury's telegram at all did you?"

"Ye... ye... yes I did," he stuttered.

"You're lying! You took her message to Ben Terrell just like you were goin' to take mine."

"He... forced me to. He sent his foreman over to see me, and he said if any of those widows came in to send a telegram, I was not to really send it off but to bring it to him. If I didn't, he said he'd... shoot me."

"Well I'm not a widow. Why were you takin' my telegram to him?"

"I saw Mr. Terrell's name mentioned, and I knew he'd pay me for the information."

"You send off Miz Tilsbury's telegram to the U.S. marshal right now, or I'll pay you, and it won't be in dollars! You got that?"

"Yes, sir."

Kenyon released his hold and the clerk spun around and sent the message out immediately.

Riley went into several saloons and asked some carefully worded questions like, "What's been goin' on out at the Circle T?" and "Have Terrell's cows quit running yet?" so he could pick up some good information for Kenyon without arousing suspicion. Getting no luck from the closed-mouth waddies at Big Alice's Horsehead Bar and the Silver Buckle, he decided to try the Buckboard at the end of the street.

Riley figured that if anyone knew what was going on at the Circle T, it would be Harlan Dowdy, the Buckboard bartender. Riley put on his best gunslinger swagger and banged open the bat-wing doors with his chest, having stuck both thumbs down inside the front of his gunbelt. "Gimme a shot of rye," he said, squinting a deadly squint at Harlan Dowdy.

When Dowdy brought the whiskey, he set the glass down in front of Riley and said, "Two bits."

Riley, still squinting, suddenly realized he couldn't see the change he held in his hand. Opening his eyes wide, he picked out a quarter and looked up at Dowdy. That was the first time he noticed Hank and Shorty in the mirror. They were standing in back of him grinning. He reached for his gun, but his hand found an empty holster.

"Did you lose somethin', kid?" Hank asked.

"Like this maybe?" Shorty said holding up Riley's gun.

Riley gulped.

"Where's that saddle-tramp pardner of yours?" Hank asked, stepping closer.

"He's back at the ranch," Riley lied.

"Ranch!" Shorty laughed. "You call that miserable two-bit farm of old lady Tilsbury's a ranch?" He threw back his head and laughed. "Ain't that a hot one, Hank? A sodbustin' squatter callin' a broken-down farm a ranch! If that don't beat all."

The asthmatic wheezer came bolting through the door waving a copy of the telegraph message he had just sent for Kenyon. "Is Mr. Terrell coming into town today?" he asked Hank. "I have something of the utmost importance to communicate to . . ."

Hank grabbed him by the coat lapels and lifted him off his feet. "I'm Mr. Terrell's right-hand man. I thought I made that clear to you when we had our little visit in your office." Then easing up slightly on his grip, he added, "Whatever you've got for him, you can give to me."

Seeing the possibility of his reward going down the drain, the clerk took a calculated risk. "I'd prefer giving it to Mr. Terrell personally."

"Would you *prefer*," Hank said stressing the word, "to strain your food through cheesecloth? 'Cause you ain't gonna have no teeth to eat with by the time I get through with you if you don't gimme that message."

The wheezer gulped and handed over Kenyon's message to the territorial governor. Hank took a while to fully digest the contents of the telegram before he spoke again, "When did he come to send this off?"

"About twenty minutes ago."

"You ain't sent it off yet, have you?"

"I had to," the clerk said whimpering.

"Why you dumb. . ."

"He forced me to!" the wheezer squeaked. "He held a gun to my head."

"You mean like this?" Shorty asked, sticking Riley's gun against the wheezer's nose.

"Ah . . . ah. . ."

"Is he sayin' huh-uh, or ha-ha, or what the hell's he sayin'?" Shorty asked Hank.

At that moment two of Hank's riders came in. Hank looked over and called one of them. "Jason, ride out to the Circle T and tell Mr. Terrell we done got a scrawny surprise package for him. And tell him Kenyon's in town sending messages to the governor. Now git!"

Jason wheeled around and ran out the door. Shorty pulled the barrel of Riley's gun out of the wheezer's nose and told the little man to get moving. Needing no encouragement, the telegraph agent flew out the door, bumping into four mean-looking hard cases who'd just stepped onto the boardwalk in front of the Buckboard. One of them sent him on his way with a flying kick in the seat of his trousers. Then they shouldered their way inside.

"There he is!" one of them shouted.

Riley suddenly felt an iron grip on the collar of his shirt. He was spun roughly around and came face-to-face with Zeke Hagan. He inhaled noisily through a wide-opened mouth as his jaw dropped and his eyes widened in terror.

Zeke grinned and glanced back over his shoulder at Carl. "Looks like your ridin' days are over, boys. We got what we came for. Come on, Riley!"

"I'd say your ridin' days ain't finished yet," Hank said. "Get your hands off this kid."

Zeke's eyes narrowed, and the corners of his mouth turned downward as his jaw muscles tightened. He relaxed his grip on Riley's shirt collar and pointed his finger at Hank. "Mister, you're buttin' into things you'd do a hell of a lot better by keepin' your nose out of. Me and my brothers have been trackin' this mangy bastard for one hell of a long time, and we ain't about to lose him again. Now we're goin' out of here, and we're takin' Riley with us. I don't think you'd better try and stop us."

Hank, who was a good three inches taller than Zeke and at least fifty pounds heavier, glared at the other three Hagans, and then let his glare come to rest on Zeke's hard face.

"If you've got some kind of beef with Riley, you're gonna have to stand in line 'cause we had him first. And by God not you nor nobody else is gonna walk in here and tell me what I can do or can't do. Now you get your ass out of here and take those ugly brothers of yours with you."

Hank edged to one side of Riley, and Shorty, still holding Riley's gun, moved away from him on the other side. Matthew, the Circle T rider who had come in with Jason, stepped to the right side of Hank so that the four of them were standing in a straight line facing the Hagans.

Zeke and Bronco were in front with Carl and Orville spread out behind them forming a wedge. Zeke studied the situation carefully. Riley was unarmed. The short guy on Riley's left was holding the gun he'd taken from Riley, and the other two on Riley's right side didn't look particularly dangerous. He gave a slight nod to Bronco, then turned around and winked at Carl and Orville.

"Alright, boys, let's go,"

They started toward the door, and then Zeke said, "Now!" They spun around as one, drawing and firing.

As soon as Zeke said "now," Riley dropped to the floor and started crawling toward a table for some protection. Shorty raised Riley's gun as the Hagans were turning and shot Carl through the side. Hank and Matthew drew and fired at the time the Hagans did. Zeke's first shot blew a hole in the edge of the bar where Riley had been standing. Hank's shot caught Zeke in his left arm before he could fire a second time and sent him reeling backwards. Orville's bullet hit Matthew in the groin and knocked him down. Matthew raised up on one elbow and shot Bronco, hitting him in the stomach. Bronco staggered backwards and fell, firing a shot into the ceiling as he did so. Shorty's next shot caught Orville in the chest and dropped him. Zeke got up from the chairs he'd crashed into and fired again. The bullet grazed Hank's left hand causing Hank's third shot to go off its mark and strike Zeke in the thigh. Zeke's leg collapsed under him and he went down.

Ed Wallace, the sheriff, came running into the Buckboard with his gun drawn. "What's goin' on here, Hank?"

"These four drifters tried to kidnap young Riley

here, and we stopped 'em. Better get Doc Weaver, Ed. Matthew's been hit bad."

Ed straightened up from where he had been inspecting Orville. "This one's dead and that one, that's gut-shot, ain't gonna make it either. The other two look like they'll pull through with some doctorin'." He picked up their guns and headed for Doc Weaver's office.

"Looks like you caused us some trouble, Riley, but we'll get you one of these days," Zeke said. Then looking at Hank and Shorty he added, "And from the looks of it, I'll add you two jaspers to the list for killin' Orville and Bronco."

Riley got up from under the table still shaking. "You're crazier than a loon, Zeke. Ain't nobody brought trouble to you 'cept yourself. I told you I didn't do nothin' to your sister. You're gonna keep it up till the whole damned bunch of you is dead . . . and good riddance."

Doc Weaver came through the door carrying his black bag. He stopped to look at Zeke first.

"Get over here, Doc, and take a look at Matthew. Never mind that sonofabitch. He's the one that started it."

"This man's bleedin' pretty bad. I'll have to stop it first."

Hank aimed his gun at Doc. "I said get over here and look at Matthew. I don't give a damn about that joker. He can bleed to death for all I care. Matthew's a-hurtin'."

Matthew groaned as if on cue and Doc Weaver got up. He was angry. These damned cowboys treated shooting someone the same way they did taking a drink of whiskey. It was part of their everyday lives. They thought no more of killing a man than they did of branding a cow. No one ever fought with their fists any more. If you disagreed with a man, you didn't try to settle the disagreement with an argument supported by facts; you pulled out your gun and killed him or left him shot up so badly he wasn't worth much afterwards.

"Take a look at my hand when you get through with Matthew, Doc. I got winged and it's bleedin'."

Doc Weaver turned on Hank. "Men like you don't bleed. You got crap in your veins." He ignored Hank's threatening glare. "Take these men to my office. I can't probe for a bullet on a barroom floor."

The saloon had begun to fill up with curious onlookers. Doc singled out four of them. "You fellas take these two wounded men up to my office, and you two carry this dead one down to Ark Fletcher's funeral parlor. And tell him he ought to get another pine box ready . . . 'cause one of these boys looks pretty bad."

Hank nodded at Shorty. "You take Riley into the back room and watch him till I get through. I'll get one of these gawkers here to help me carry Matthew. Hey, you!" he yelled at a man who was staring open-mouthed at Zeke, "come give me a hand, and we'll carry this fella down to the Doc's office."

As they moved out, Shorty nudged Riley with his own gun. "Let's go into the back room, kid. That way we can have a nice quiet conversation till Hank gets back, and you can tell me how in the hell Kenyon can be back at the 'ranch' and still be in the telegraph office at the same time."

14

KENYON HAD HEARD THE SHOTS, BUT THEY were muffled and sounded quite far away. He wondered about them, but Hank and Shorty wouldn't have wasted that many taking Riley. He rode over to Clinton's Livery Stable on a hunch and spotted Hank's and Shorty's horses in the stalls. The hoslter told him that the horses had been there for three days. Hank and Shorty wouldn't be hangin' around for so long unless they were here for a very good reason, he thought. They're waitin' for either Riley or me to come ridin' in unsuspectin', and then they'll make their move. He left his horse at the stable and headed toward the telegraph office.

Tom Nathan, the town busybody, never let an opportunity go by to corner a listener and tell a juicy shoot-out story. He spotted Kenyon and crossed the street beaming. Seeing a listener coming from the opposite end of town, Nathan knew he was unaware of the great event. So he opened his greeting with, "Say, that was some shoot-out, wasn't it?"

Kenyon stopped and looked at Nathan up and down. He didn't look like the kind of man who hung around saloons, and that's where most gunfights started . . . and ended. He then figured that what he was about to hear was a second-hand story. "What shoot-out? I haven't heard about it."

This was music to Nathan's ears. He could hardly

contain himself as he started. "Well . . . down at the Buckboard—"

"Did you see any of this, or is it all third-hand information?" Kenyon interrupted; then, he flashed a wry grin.

Tom puffed up what chest he had and smiled smugly. "I arrived on the scene at the very same instant Dr. Weaver did. We nearly went through the door together. I was—"

"If Doc Weaver was there, the shootin' was all over with," Kenyon said. "So that would make it ah . . . third-hand information."

Nathan showed visible irritation and would have continued on his journey, letting Kenyon hear the news from someone else, but that idea was even more irritating than Kenyon's interruption and snide comment, so he chose to ignore both and started the story again. "When I got there, two men were dead and three men were wounded, if you exclude the little bullet-crease Hank got. Myself, of course, I'd hardly call it a—"

"Did you say Hank? Terrell's foreman?" Kenyon asked, suddenly getting interested.

Nathan knew that he'd hooked his listener. It bothered him that Kenyon had interrupted again, but he could feel that warm feeling growing inside. It always came when he had charmed a listener into hearing one of his stories. "Yes, it was Hank, foreman of the Circle T. Anyways, it seems that four men came into the Buckboard and got into an argument with Hank and Shorty and another Circle T rider. They started blazing away at each other, and it wound up with two of the brothers dead, one very badly wounded and one with an arm and a leg shot up. The Circle T rider was hit in the—"

"Did you say these four hombres were brothers?"

Nathan could feel the anger another interruption was bringing, and he fought to keep it under control.

"Yes," he hissed through clenched teeth. "I believe the one that was shot in the leg and the arm said their name was Higgins or Hagan or something like that."

"Hagan!" Kenyon exclaimed. "The Hagan brothers. Did you see a lanky young kid named Riley in the Buckboard at all?"

Nathan gave Kenyon a look of disdain. "I didn't notice any of the *bystanders*."

Kenyon grabbed Nathan's coat lapel. "He wouldn't be a bystander. He would have been involved in it, the *cause* of it most likely. Did you see him?"

Nathan squirmed uncomfortably. "Well," he gulped to moisten his dry throat, "there was a slim young man standing near the bar. The last time I saw him, he was heading for the back room, he and Shorty. I guess they're waiting for—"

"Thanks a lot, pardner. You really tell a good story."

Tom's momentary anger at still another interruption was pushed aside by Kenyon's compliment. He hooked his thumbs in his vest. "Well, thank you." He put his nose in the air and continued talking. "I do pride myself on being a good—" Kenyon was already a half-dozen paces away and moving fast. "A good observer!" Tom shouted finishing his sentence. "Illiterate cowhand. Probably doesn't even know the meaning of the word." He adjusted his tie and continued walking down the street, looking for a new listener.

Helen was just putting the last of her supplies into the wagon when Kenyon arrived. "You boys about ready to go?"

"Hank and Shorty have Riley in the back room of Terrell's saloon."

"Terrell's saloon?"

"The Buckboard."

"Now what do you suppose they're goin' to do with that boy?"

"I don't think they'll do too much to him. I think they'll use him mainly to force me to ride out to the Circle T and give myself up."

"They'd kill you if you do."

"And they'll kill Riley if I don't. I've got to get him out of there if I can."

"Looks like the big man himself," Helen said, "comin' in with all his boys."

Kenyon looked down the street and saw Ben Terrell riding at the head of a group of eight horsemen. To keep from being seen as Terrell rode by, Kenyon ducked down by the side of Helen's wagon.

Terrell glared at Helen as he passed and then turned the corner and rode out of sight. When the Circle T riders had disappeared, Kenyon straightened up.

"He'll find out I'm in town soon enough. Why don't you go on home, and I'll join you as soon as I get Riley safely out of that back room."

"Ain't there nothin' I can do to help?"

"No, you go on now, and we'll be home pretty soon."

Helen put her hand on his arm. "You watch yourself and be careful, Kenyon. I'd hate to lose my hired help. I've kind of gotten used to you two jaybirds."

Kenyon smiled and patted her hand. "We'll be home before long. You go ahead."

Helen climbed up on the wagon seat and started out of town. Kenyon watched until she had turned the corner. Then, he headed for the Buckboard.

He studied the building in the fading light of early evening. It was a two-story affair with a saloon occupying the bottom floor and smaller rooms in the second story, most likely used by the barmaids when they found a willing and able cowhand with money in his pockets.

Kenyon found a lantern hanging on the back wall of Dunstan's Hardware Store and took it with him. He walked up the back stairs of the Buckboard and eased through the door. Creeping quietly down the hall, he stopped and listened outside each door. Satisfied that there was no one in any of the rooms, he poured a stream of coal oil down the hallway from one end to the other. Then he continued dribbling the coal oil down the stairs until he stood on the bottom step. Pulling a match from his pocket, he started to strike it with his thumbnail, but suddenly stopped.

I guess I'd better find out exactly where they've got Riley first; then, I'll set this place on fire, he thought.

Two cowboys came riding up the street, so Kenyon ducked under the stairs until they had passed. Setting the lantern down against the wall, he moved along the back of the building until he reached the rear door. He turned the knob slowly and opened the door several inches. The sound of voices jumbled together came like a thunderclap as the speakers raised their volume. He could easily pick out Hank's and Terrell's voices from the rest of the mumbling.

"You know how much money you and that damned Kenyon have cost me in the last month?" Terrell asked.

Riley didn't answer.

"It's 'cause of you that Matthew took a bullet in the belly, and I got shot in the hand!" Hank shouted. "You ain't done nothin' but cause misery and trouble since you first rode into town. We ought to string you up right now!" There came a sound of a hand slapping flesh.

"We ought to, but we need you alive for awhile at least," Terrell added. "We've got to smoke Kenyon out, and you're gonna help us do it."

Kenyon backed out and closed the door. You're the one that's goin' to be smoked out, he thought. Moving quickly back to the stairs, he climbed again to the second floor and threw several lit matches onto the coal-oil-soaked wood. The dry walls and flooring exploded into flames. Kenyon went quickly to the back stairs and set them afire. Then he ran back to the rear door and waited. It was almost five minutes before smoke from the second floor drifted into the bar.

Someone yelled "Fire! Fire!" and the backroom emptied as the men ran down the hall and through the front door to the horse trough outside. Several men ran into Dunstan's Hardware, picked up some buckets, and began forming a brigade.

Kenyon stepped into the hallway and moved down toward the bar until he came to the room where Riley was held prisoner. He felt a burst of anger as he saw Riley's face. The kid had been beaten pretty badly, but he was still conscious. When Kenyon called his name softly, Riley looked up and his battered lips parted into a big grin.

"I knowed you'd find out where I was."

Kenyon cut the ropes binding Riley's arms and legs to the chair and helped him to his feet. "Let's get out of here," he urged.

As they stepped to the door, they almost bumped head-on into Shorty who was just coming into the room. Taken completely by surprise, he gawked at them openmouthed for a second, then reached for his gun. Riley swung his bony fist with all the pent-up fury and hate he'd stored since he had been caught and beaten. It hit Shorty flush on the nose, and the ridge snapped like a dry cottonwood twig. Shorty staggered backwards until his shoulders hit the wall; then, he slid slowly to the floor and fell sideways, blood gushing out of his broken nose.

Riley's jaw sagged open in astonishment. "Well I'll be danged."

"Come on," Kenyon urged. "Move!"

They went out the rear door at a run. The street in front was filled with people yelling and dipping buckets into the horse trough. The whole second story was a blazing inferno, and the walls of the ground floor were showing yellow-red flames along the top half.

Kenyon and Riley made it to the livery stable without being seen. Kenyon took his horse out of the stall, and he and Riley mounted up double and headed for Helen's place.

She met them at the door when they rode into the yard.

"You two jaybirds are sure a sigh fer sore eyes. Come on inside. I've got some stew a-cookin' on the— Good Lord A'mighty! What did they do to you, boy? Looks like they took to your face with a razor strap. It's all puffed up and cut to smithereens. Come sit down and let me look at that mess."

Riley sat down and grinned. "Kenyon and me showed 'em. He set fire to the Buckboard, and I broke Shorty's nose. Best danged night I've had in a coon's age."

Kenyon smiled. "Yeah, he was enjoyin' it so much, he didn't even want to come home with me."

Helen shook her head. "Both of you yahoos are gonna wind up blown to hell in some canyon somewheres, and it'll be my fault. Maybe I ought to just pack up and move out. No use you boys gettin' killed 'count of me."

Kenyon winked at Riley. "Yeah, that sounds like you, Helen, turnin' chicken in the middle of a fight and runnin' off."

"I ain't turnin' chicken," she growled. "It's just that . . . well . . . you two are the nearest things I've ever had to sons, and I don't want you gittin' shot up over me."

"Hell, I ain't doin' it for you, Helen," Kenyon said, "I kinda had my eyes on Alpha."

Helen threw back her head and roared with laughter. "I'm keepin' what you said right here." She tapped the side of her head with one finger. "And if you don't walk a straight line, I'm tellin' her exactly what you said."

Kenyon sat down next to Riley. "There ain't nothin' more devious than a woman's mind, Kid. Let this be a lesson to you."

Helen's laughter died, and her face became serious again. "I've thought about it . . . about maybe movin' out and lettin' Terrell have the whole kit and kaboodle. If I had someplace to go, I'd shuck the whole thing. But, I ain't got nothin' 'cept this house. It ain't big enough to cuss a coyote in without gettin' hair in your teeth, but it's home to me, and I'd hate like the devil to have that horse's ass Terrell drive me out."

"Don't worry, Helen. Nobody's gonna drive you anywhere . . . especially Terrell," Kenyon said.

"Yeah," Riley put in, "me and Kenyon will protect you, Miz Tilsbury. You got two good men right here." He slapped his leg for emphasis.

Kenyon looked at Riley's puffed and swollen face, then turned and winked at Helen. "A real tiger. I wish I had a dozen more just like him."

Riley wore a grin that refused to die even when Helen dabbed some stinging ointment on his battered face.

She just tightened her mouth some to help hold back the tears and sniffed loudly.

Ben Terrell stood coatless and sweat-soaked, staring at the smoking embers of his once-thriving Buckboard Saloon. Although no one had talked about it, he knew that Kenyon must have started the blaze. Someone had pulled an unconscious and slightly scorched Shorty out of the hallway just before it exploded into flame. When the little man had come to, he told of meeting Kenyon and Riley in the back room. Shorty said that both men jumped him and that Kenyon had kicked him in the face while he was down. He vowed to get revenge.

"The line forms in the rear," Terrell had told him. "I *owe* that man, and I aim to *pay him back*."

"What are we gonna do now, boss?" Hank asked, as Terrell surveyed the wreckage.

"I'm gonna send a wire," Terrell replied.

"To the governor?"

"Hell no! I'm sendin' a wire to John Haskins in Flagstaff. I'm gonna tell him to send me the best gunfighter he can find."

"You need a gunfighter just to run them women off the land?" Hank asked.

Terrell spun around angrily. "I want him to get rid of Kenyon and Riley. You and the rest of the Circle T riders have made a mess of things. I started out with a full crew, and all I've got now is a bunch of cripples, a herd that ain't got enough meat on their bones to stuff a baby buzzard, and a pile of black kindlin' wood where a damned good money-makin' saloon stood just three hours ago. What I need is a good strong man to do a job that's been needing to be done for too damned long."

"I wish you'd give me another chance, Mr. Terrell," Hank said, kicking at a live coal that had popped off a smoldering board.

"I said I needed a strong man to do the job. You and the rest of the Circle T bunch together ain't strong enough to pull a sick whore off a pee pot!" Terrell thundered. "Now get on over to Doc Weaver's and see if Shorty's able to ride while I go send a telegram."

"Yes sir," Hank mumbled.

15

BEN TERRELL LOOKED UP OVER THE TOP OF the telegram he'd just received and smiled at Hank. "You know who's comin' to take care of Kenyon and Riley for us? A Texas gunman named Wingate. Ever hear of him?"

Hank's jaw sagged, causing his mouth to drop open in amazement. "You mean E. J. Wingate?"

Terrell's smile broadened into a grin that exposed his yellowish uneven teeth. He nodded.

Hank let out a long whistle. "He's supposed to be about the meanest and the fastest gunfighter that ever sat on a horse."

"If you're going to hire someone to work for you, you might as well get the best. It'll save a lot of time and headaches in the long run," Terrell said.

"When's he comin' in?"

Terrell folded the telegram and put in into his desk. "He'll be here in a week."

Hank chuckled. "Man, that's gonna be somethin' to see, E. J. Wingate in a shootout. Wait till I tell the boys about this." He rose to leave.

"That might not be a good idea, Hank. There could be some trouble stirred up on account of that wire Kenyon sent to the territorial governor. If there is, I don't want people in town to know I've got a hired gun workin' for me. Let's just keep this under our hats for awhile."

"Whatver you say, boss." He walked out and headed for the bunkhouse. Once inside he moved up to Shorty's bunk. "Hey, Shorty," he said quietly.

Shorty rolled over and stared at Hank. His face was still raw from the burns. Both eyes were black, and there was a heavy band of blackish purple that went over the flattened bridge of his nose and connected the two discolored, puffy eyes. A large cotton ball was stuffed inside each nostril; they were soiled with dirt and dried blood and needed to be replaced. "What do you want?" he mumbled thickly.

Hank looked over both of his shoulders to make sure no one was close enough to hear him. Then, sitting down on the bed next to Shorty, he said, "Do you know what the boss is gonna do to stop Kenyon and Riley?"

"How in the hell would I know?" Shorty grumbled. "I ain't been off this bed 'cept to go to the pot for the last three days."

Hank ignored Shorty's grousing and glanced over both shoulders again. Lowering his voice to a whisper, he continued. "Terrell's bringin' in a hired gun. Know who it is?"

"Goddamnit, Hank, you got somethin' to tell me, get it said. I can't abide no guessin' games."

"Sh!" Hank whispered. "Keep your voice down. Mr. Terrell wants this information kept secret. Didn't even want me to tell you about it. He's bringin' in none other than the famous Mr. E. J. Wingate from San Anton', Texas."

Shorty's eyes burned beneath swollen lids. "It's prob'bly costin' him a fortune to hire Wingate. Why in the hell don't he give me and you a chance? We could do it for half the price. In face, I'll kill Riley for nothin' and throw in Kenyon to boot."

Hank looked glum. "He says we ain't good enough. Says he wants a strong man to do the job."

"What in the hell's so all-fired strong about Wingate? Has he got muscles in his crap or somethin'? Alls he can do is fast draw, and that ain't worth a sly fart in church if the other feller don't play the game with you. Soon as my nose and eyes get well, give me a Winchester, and I'll blow both of 'em to hell."

Hank grinned. "*If* Wingate misses, which I *know* will not be the case, you and me will get our chance."

"Ain't nothin' in this world I'd like more than to grind Riley's face into the dirt with my boot heel," Shorty said. "As a matter of fact, that goes for his pardner too." For a moment Hank thought he saw a light smile spreading through the hills and ridges of Shorty's distorted features.

Kenyon guided the line-back dun along the back streets until he came to Herman Konig's blacksmith shop; then, he stopped and eased out of the saddle. Leaving the horse tied to a hitching rail at the rear entrance near Konig's forge, he stepped inside. Herman looked up and smiled.

"How's dat big plow I sell you doing? Tearing up lots of ground?"

Kenyon grinned. "Riley's the plow jockey. That ain't exactly my kind of work, but from what I've seen, it's holdin' up real good. Many Circle T riders in town?"

"I don't see any since the big fire. I guess they got plenty of work at Terrell's ranch. Something strange going on. I tell you."

Kenyon's expression firmed up. "What do you mean?"

"Eli says a famous gunshooter's coming to town."

"Who's Eli?"

"He's the telegram clerk."

"Oh, yeah," Kenyon replied, "the little wheezer. Who's this famous gent comin' in, a U.S. marshal?"

"Don't know." Herman shrugged. "He just say E. J. . . . somebody . . . very famous man is coming."

Kenyon ran the initials E. J. through his mind and came up with a blank. "Well, Eli is the man I came in town to see. I'll ask him about it. That horse won't be in your way, will it? I kind of wanted to keep him off the streets for awhile."

Herman waved a thick arm. "Not to worry. He's fine."

Kenyon nodded a thanks and headed for the telegraph office. Eli Cardwell was alone when Kenyon stepped inside. He was busy reading again and didn't bother to look up. "Pencil and paper's on the counter. I'll be with you in a minute."

"Haven't you finished reading that story yet?" Kenyon asked.

Eli recognized Kenyon's voice, and he bounded out of the chair dropping his magazine as he did so. "Yes sir, yes sir, what can I do for you?"

"Two things. First, I want to know if I've received a telegram from the governor's office. It's been over two weeks now, and I could have ridden there and delivered it by hand in that length of time."

Eli's mouth developed a nervous twitch in the right hand corner. "Ah . . . no sir . . . ah . . . nothing's come in yet."

Kenyon grabbed the front of Eli's coat with his left hand and lifted the little man's feet a good eighteen inches off the floor. "I don't believe you heard me right, Eli. I said it's been over two weeks, and I know the governor wouldn't keep me hanging around this long for an answer. You want to tell me again if I have a telegram waiting for me?"

"Well . . . ah . . . ," he gulped, "there was a message that came in about a week or so ago. Mr. Terrell said that any messages for you were to be sent directly to him. He said he'd see to it that you got everything that was coming to you."

"That sounds like Terrell," Kenyon said relaxing hig grip. "Tell me, Eli, do you have any idea what the prison sentence is for someone who monkeys around with United States mail? I figure what you did with my telegram—you know, giving it to another person— I figure that ought to buy you enough time in the Yuma Territorial Prison to make you about ten years older than Pittsburgh by the time you get out."

Eli Cardwell began to shake like a drunk with the D.T.'s. He tried to speak, but as usual his only sound was a familiar, monotonous, "ah."

Kenyon dropped him back down to the floor but retained his hold on the little man's coat. "Do you remember what the message said?"

With his feet on solid flooring once again, Eli regained some of his composure. "It . . . ah . . . it said that a U.S. marshal was on his way."

"What did Terrell do about that?"

"He sent a message to the governor saying that all the trouble had been cleared up, and that the marshal wasn't needed after all."

"That's mighty nice of you to share my message with Ben Terrell. When did he send off this telegram?"

"Just yesterday. I guess the fire took his mind off the governor. I suppose with Mr. E. J. Wingate coming in, he felt the town didn't need any marshal."

"Who's E. J. Wingate?"

"He's one of the fastest guns in the West. I just read an article about him in *Harper's*."

"Mr. Cardwell, I've got to hand it to you. You made a brilliant observation there. If Terrell's gettin' a hired gun to do his fightin' for him, there's no need for a marshal to come buttin' in. After all, by the time that gunslinger's finished shootin' all the people who hate

Ben Terrell, there won't be anyone in this town left to break the law . . . 'cept maybe you, and I wouldn't count on your being around. Now you pick up that pencil 'cause I've got another message for you to send. Address it to the territorial governor. Say: 'The situation has gotten worse. We will need a law man after all. Disregard my previous message to you, and send a U.S. marshal immediately. Signed—Respectfully yours, Ben Terrell, Circle T Ranch.'"

"I . . . can't do that. It's against the law."

"Listen, you little worm. You've already broken the law enough to keep you bustin' rocks for the next forty years. You send that telegram right now, or you won't be able to send another one ever 'cause I'll break both your arms."

"Yes sir!"

Eli sent the message without further delay.

Kenyon turned and started for the door but stopped and stared at Eli one more time. "If I were you, Eli, I do believe I'd think long and hard about my bein' in here tonight. As a matter of fact, I don't think I'd tell a soul about it . . . if I were you . . . Eli." He opened the door and stepped into the darkness.

The ride back to Helen's gave Kenyon plenty of time to digest what Eli had said. So Terrell had hired a gunslinger to fight for the Circle T. That was bad. Kenyon felt that he could hold his own with most of the gunfighters he'd seen in the past, but now that he'd thought about the name E. J. Wingate a little more, he realized that he had heard of the man; in fact, he had seen Wingate up in Colorado. He'd shot four men up there, and was known to be a ruthless killer. And he was fast. The story was that each of the four men he'd shot had drawn first, but their guns had never cleared leather. Wingate had plugged them while they were still drawing. Kenyon knew that when he'd have to face Wingate—and there was no doubt in his mind that the time would come—he would have to have an edge. *That* would be a difficult thing to accomplish. A gunfighter like E. J. Wingate never let anyone have an advantage. That's what kept him alive. That's what gave him the confidence he needed. If Kenyon could get Wingate rattled long enough to make him lose his concentration, even for a second, the distraction would give Kenyon the edge he needed. But how do you distract a gunfighter with a reputation like E. J. Wingate? He had probably seen every ruse in the books tried at one time or another. Well, Kenyon thought, it's somethin' to think about. Maybe I'll come up with a plan I can use. I guess Riley could help me. He's got a good imagination!

He could see the faint glow of a kerosene lamp lending a golden touch to Helen's window as he rode into the yard. Kenyon unsaddled the dun and turned him into the corral. Helen and Riley were waiting for him at the door. When he stepped inside, he noticed Alpha sitting at the table having coffee.

"Well?" Helen looked at him closely. "Did you find out about the telegram?"

Kenyon nodded. "Yeah, I found out. Hello, Alpha. I didn't see your rig out there."

"Lydia brought me out. I'm spending the night. What you been up to in town?"

"I felt we should have had an answer to the telegram I sent to the governor, so I went in to find out."

"And?" she asked.

"Mr. Eli Cardwell, the telegraph clerk hand delivered it to Ben Terrell. Terrell told him he'd make sure that I'd get everything I had comin' to me."

"Sounds just like somethin' that sidewinder would say, don't it, Helen," Alpha commented.

"Sure does. What gits me is why did that dried-up little fart give Terrell your telegram in the first place? He ain't got no business doin' that."

"That's against the law, ain't it Kenyon?" Riley asked.

"I think so. At least I told Cardwell it was, and I also told him I'd send him to the Yuma Territorial Prison if he breathed a word about my bein' in town askin' questions."

"I bet that made him shake a bit," Riley said chuckling.

Helen pointed to a chair. "Sit down, and I'll git you some coffee." After pouring him a cup and refilling the others, she continued. "Well, what you gonna do about that telegram?"

"I've already done it," Kenyon answered. "Terrell sent a telegram telling the governor to cancel sending a U.S. marshal out to investigate. So I sent one to the governor and told him things have gotten worse and to disregard the previous telegram and to send us a marshal right away, and I signed it Ben Terrell."

"Good fer you," Helen said laughing. "Ain't that a pipper!"

"That's not all," Kenyon continued. "He also sent for a hired gun named Wingate."

Riley gulped. "You mean E. J. Wingate, the famous gunfighter?"

"The same."

"Oh, jeez!" Riley exclaimed. "What are we gonna do, Kenyon? We can't fight the likes of him. That guy's faster than a bullet from what I've heard."

"I guess we heard from the same source," Kenyon said. "Well, I figure it this way. The man's human, which means he's got a weakness. I'll have to find out what it is."

"Them kind that hire out to do somebody's killin' for him, ain't human at all. They're a bunch of damn vultures that feed off the dead," Helen commented. "He prob'bly won't give you any time to figure him out anyways. He'll back-shoot you 'fore you can blink an eye."

"I don't think Wingate will do any back-shootin'," Kenyon added. "He's got a reputation to live up to. He'll figure anybody could back-shoot, so why send for him if they didn't want to see a show. No, he'll call me out, and it won't be back in a canyon somewheres. It'll be right in the middle of town where everyone can see what happens to a man who goes against Terrell's grain."

"Then you and Riley git packed up and git out of here while the gittin's good," Helen said.

Kenyon smiled at Helen's serious expression. "I'm not goin' anywhere, Helen. Riley and I can take a dozen hired guns like Wingate any day of the week. Isn't that right, Kid? All we have to do is figure some way to distract him for a second or two."

"Why heckfire," Riley said, swelling out his chest. "We'll work out a plan that'll swamp him with so much lead he'll think the Seventh Cavalry is usin' him for target practice."

"You said a minute ago that the two of you couldn't go up against the likes of Wingate," Alpha said.

"I was forgettin' how good Kenyon is, and that he prob'bly has a plan already worked out. That's what I was forgettin'."

"I don't like it!" Helen countered. "I don't want you boys gittin' all shot up on account of us."

"You're puttin' the plow before the horse, Helen," Kenyon answered. "I aim to talk again to the other homesteaders that are still left around here, and see if I can get some support. There's got to be some of those men who'll reconsider and stand up and fight as a group. Otherwise they'll be driven off one by one."

"Oh, we can talk to 'em again if you like, but it won't do no good. Once they find out Terrell's hired a gunfighter they'll put two and two together. Now it don't take much brains to figure out that the Circle T wasn't havin' any trouble at all pushin' out the farmers they wanted pushed out until you two jaybirds came into town. They'll realize, in very short order, that the hired gun was hired to get you two, and they'll want no part of it. They'll figure it's your fight, not theirs," Helen said.

Riley looked at Kenyon for a reaction. It didn't take long for Kenyon to see the wisdom of Helen's accurate observation of the situation. He grimaced and glanced at Riley, shaking his head. "She's right, damn it. This is our fight, Kid. Or more honestly, it's *my* fight. I was the one who thought up the dynamite trick, and it was me that burned down Terrell's saloon."

"You can't face E. J. Wingate all by your lonesome," Riley said. "Besides, you saved my life a couple times, so I owe you. You leave it to me. I'll take care of distractin' that bugger."

"What are you gonna do?" Kenyon asked, squinting at Riley.

A grin forced its way through Riley's battered face. "Don't you worry none, I got me an idea. It's a surefire humdinger."

Kenyon looked sternly at Riley. "You stay out of it, Kid. I was only kiddin' when I said that *we* could take care of a dozen hired guns like E. J. Wingate. I'll do this one alone. This ain't the kind of guy you can make a mistake with." He rose and said goodnight to Helen and Alpha. Then, with Riley close on his heels, they left.

"I think we ought to get the girls together and give Kenyon a hand, Helen. He's gonna be goin' up against a professional killer, and he won't stand any more of a chance of gittin' out of it alive than a snowball has on a hot tin roof in the middle of July, lessen we help him out."

"You're right, Alpha. We'll talk to ever'body tomorrow, including the families."

"But you said. . ."

"Forget what I said," Helen interrupted. "The more I think on it, the madder I git. All them able-bodied men lettin' a couple of boys down who don't have no stake in the land and a hand full of dried-up old prunes like us do their fightin' for 'em. They'll stand up and help us save them two boys or I swear, Alpha, I'll help Terrell drive 'em off their land myself."

Ben Terrell settled back in his chair and stared at E. J. Wingate. The man's reputation rode point wherever he went and always arrived well ahead of the man himself. Terrell was surprised at Wingate's appearance. If you could separate this hombre's eyes from the rest of him, you'd take him for a lawyer or maybe a doctor, Terrell thought. Wingate's light blue eyes were deceiving. They were an interesting combination of innocence coupled with the intent gaze of a tracker who never missed a sign. They were wide open and quick in the way they absorbed everything around him. He was completely sure of himself and gave no ground before Terrell's persistent stare. Moving down from the face, he didn't have particularly broad shoulders. In fact, he seemed on the slim side to Terrell. He was a man of average height and might easily pass for an average man on the street except for the tools of his trade and the way he wore them. He carried two Colt .45 single-action revolvers with black barrels and black gutta-percha handle grips. They rested in two black, tooled-leather holsters that were well-oiled and tied low on the legs with black leather thongs. There were only two types of men who carried two guns on their hips. One was the greenhorn cowboy who wanted to show off; an experienced hand would never need two and didn't care for the extra weight. The other was a hired gun who most likely was as good a shot with his left hand as he was with his right and wanted the edge just in case. Terrell knew that Wingate was no greenhorn.

Satisfied with his inspection of the gunfighter, Terrell got up and moved to his liquor cabinet. He poured two drinks without asking whether or not Wingate wanted one. He was used to thinking for others, and Wingate, with all his reputation, was still a hired hand. He handed a glass to the gunman and took a drink from his own glass before he spoke. "How much did John Haskins tell you about my problem?"

"He didn't. He said to see you, and you'd fill me in on what the expect."

Terrell grunted an acknowledgement of Wingate's words. Then, after he'd drained his glass, he began telling Wingate the whole rotten mess of what had happened in his life since the arrival of Kenyon and Riley. By the time he'd finished his story, his temper had risen to a point where he was nearly shouting.

E. J. Wingate's face remained almost unchanged except for a slight smile that developed at the of Terrell's narrative. He had little tolerance for men who couldn't keep their emotions in check. It was no wonder Terrell was unable to solve a simple problem like killing two cowboy troublemakers. This was going to be an easy thousand-dollar fee to earn. Riley posed no threat at all, and Kenyon—well, he might be an interesting opponent but certainly not one to lose sleep over.

"I want them killed right away," Terrell said pouring himself another drink.

"It'll be done by the end of this week," Wingate said.

"Hell, this is Tuesday. That's four or five days from now. How come so long?"

Wingate sipped his drink slowly and studied Terrell's florid face. "Mister, in my business you soon learn not to rush things. If you do, you ain't gonna be around for long. I want to look the man over, figure him out, judge what kind of fighter he is. When I'm satisfied, then I'll kill him."

"Well, he ain't no coward," Terrell said. "He held off my whole crew while he helped Riley get away from here."

Wingate grinned for the first time. "I like a man to be a bit of a challenge. Otherwise, it's like ducks in a barrel."

"I can guarantee you one thing," Terrell said, pouring his third drink. "It sure as hell ain't gonna be no duck shoot."

"I think you're underestimating me," Wingate said, his grin diminishing to a thin slit of a smile.

"I guess I am at that," Terrell countered, loosening up as the tension of repeating a very aggravating story began to ebb. He raised his half-empty glass in a toast. "Here's to good fortune for both of us."

Wingate nodded and drained his glass.

16

KENYON PULLED THE BUCKBOARD UP IN front of Brownlee's store and tethered the horse. Stepping inside, he handed Brownlee a supply list. "Would you fill this for me? Either set it in the buckboard, or put it by the door, and I'll load it when I get back."

Brownlee took the list and nodded. He hadn't liked Kenyon ever since the day Kenyon and Helen had taken the barbed wire from his back room. It was wire that had been promised to Mr. Terrell, and Terrell had been furious with him for allowing it to be taken by Kenyon. His pride still hurt from the stinging rebuke Terrell had bestowed on him, and he had not forgiven Kenyon for bringing it on. He'd fill the order, he decided, because it was good business, but he'd be damned if he was going to load it into the buckboard for Kenyon. The man could load it himself if he wanted it done.

Kenyon stopped in at the Drover Saloon to have a beer while Brownlee filled his order. There was the usual light midday crowd, a couple of cowboys in town on errands, a businessman who had sneaked away from his office or shop to have a noontime beer, and two worn barmaids. He stepped to the bar and ordered a drink. As he was taking his first sip, E. J. Wingate came in and ordered a beer. Wingate stood at the bar about ten feet away.

"That'll be fifteen cents," the bartender said.

Wingate took a half-dollar from his pocket without taking his eyes off Kenyon and dropped it on the bar. "Keep it," he said. The bartender thanked him and moved away.

Kenyon didn't know for sure if the man staring at him was Wingate or not, but he felt strongly that it was, since the man was wearing two .45s. He had seen Wingate once before, but it had been several years ago, and the light in the saloon had been bad. Wingate's staring bothered him. "You figure I'm wearin' somethin' that belongs to you, fella?"

Wingate was a little surprised at the question, but he didn't show it. "No," he said slowly drawing out the word. "If you were, it wouldn't fit me anyhow. Your name Kenyon?"

"Who's askin'?"

"My name's E. J. Wingate."

"Oh yeah, the hired murderer Terrell bought and paid for."

Wingate's face flushed a slight tinge of red as the small crowd in the saloon sat in silence listening to their conversation. They had stopped talking on the mention of his name. That warmed him a little. At least they knew who he was. Not one to be bested by an ordinary cowboy, he said, "Not a murderer. The men I've killed all drew first. Self-defense."

"Yeah, self-defense," Kenyon said. "It's like killing a blind widow that's holding a rifle. You can always claim she pulled a gun on you."

"You got a wise mouth, Kenyon. I'm surprised you've lived this long."

"That makes two of us that are surprised. You'd figure a snake with a reputation like yours would have been blown away by now."

"It'll take more than a big mouth like you to do it," Wingate said straightening up. "What makes you so sure I won't just kill you right now?"

Kenyon smiled and took the last swallow of beer in his glass before answering. "I don't figure you've got enough of a crowd. Besides that, I think you'll want your boss here to see what kind of *thing* it is he hired." He touched his fingers to the brim of his hat in a salute and smiled. "See ya." He turned his back to Wingate and headed for the door.

Wingate was furious, but Kenyon had figured him out perfectly. He didn't want to kill Kenyon in a saloon with only a couple of barmaids and three rummies sitting around staring at him. He wanted to take him on the main street where the whole town could see what a beautiful killing machine he really was. That was how reputations and legends were made. The more people that saw a shoot-out, the more exaggerated the stories became, and *he* would be the main character, the fearless hero in the stories. He smiled and felt the tension ebb as he gained control again. "You have until Sunday noon, Kenyon," he called as Kenyon reached the door. "If you're not here, I'll ride out and drag you away from that old woman's skirts." Then he laughed.

Kenyon walked outside and turned in the direction of Brownlee's store. He suddenly let out the breath he had held for so long. Both hands were shaking, and beads of perspiration had popped out on his forehead. Wingate was a cool one, but Kenyon felt he had put a small burr under the man's hide. He knew he had shaken a little of Wingate's confidence by seeming to be so self-assured. By showing disdain for the man and heaping contempt on him in front of witnesses, he had put a small shadow of doubt in Wingate's mind. That might be enough to make him fire the first shot too fast and provide that very slim edge Kenyon hoped he could get.

He paid Brownlee the money for the supplies, then loaded them into the buckboard and drove home.

* * *

Riley was standing by the corral waiting as he drove up. "Boy, I'm glad to see you're still in one piece. I sure 'nuff figured they'd be a-waitin' fer you in town. I was about ready to saddle up and ride in to give you a hand. Anything happen?"

"Not much. I met E. J. Wingate in the Drover while I was gettin' a beer."

"You mean he just came up and introduced himself? Why didn't he kill you? I mean . . . I'm glad he didn't . . . but I don't understand."

"Well," Kenyon said, unhooking the horse from the buckboard and turning it into the corral, "he just came in and stood next to me and bought a beer. He asked if I was Kenyon, and I said yes. He said he was E. J. Wingate, and he told me I had until Sunday noon. He said if I didn't come into town then, he would come out here and drag me out from behind Helen's skirt."

"He sure don't lack for gall, does he?" Helen said, stepping up behind him.

"No . . . he doesn't," Kenyon said, drawing out the statement. "He's a cool one, but I think I may have rattled his cage a wee bit."

"What did you do?" Riley asked, full of curiosity.

"We just talked," Kenyon replied, glossing over the incident.

"What are you plannin' to do about Sunday?" Helen asked.

"I'm goin' to meet him. I sure don't want him ridin' out here."

"You could ride out for points unknown and leave all this mess behind," she suggested.

"You ought to know me better than that, Helen. I'll not run from any man, and that includes E. J. Wingate. Besides, maybe I'll get lucky."

"Well you sure can count on me to be a-helpin' you . . . if you need me," Riley said.

"Where is the big shoot-out supposed to take place?" she asked.

"Right in front of the Drover Saloon where the whole town can see what a fast gunslinger Wingate really is."

"Well, come on in and have some coffee 'fore the mosquitos carry us into the next county."

Helen asked no more questions, but it was clear to Kenyon that she was brooding about the situation. Riley was a different case entirely. He talked incessantly on every aspect of the coming gunplay except for one thing. He refused to promise not to get involved. All he would admit to was the fact that he *might* be involved. Kenyon knew that Riley had planned something that would take Wingate's mind off killing for a few seconds. It was during those precious seconds that Kenyon hoped he would be able to draw and shoot E. J. before the roles were reversed. Of course, Riley could get himself shot in a very big hurry if he did something foolish. The thought continued to plague Kenyon all through the night.

Sunday seemed to have arrived on wings. Kenyon couldn't remember days passing so quickly. After breakfast was over, he hitched up the wagon for Helen. She had lots of running around to do, picking up all of her friends to take them to church before the services began, and she wanted to leave early. Riley was still close-mouthed about his plans, so Kenyon cleaned and oiled his gun. He even practiced a few quick-draws just to loosen up a bit. At eleven o'clock he saddled the line-back dun while Riley did the same with his horse, and the two of them headed for town. Neither of them said anything until they reached the city limits. Kenyon broke their silence.

"I don't know what you've got planned, Kid, but remember that gunslingers like E. J. Wingate are still alive because they're wise to every trick in the book.

You mess with that man and you'll get yourself killed.''

"They ain't seen ever' trick," Riley said grinning.

"You've also got to remember that Hank and Shorty are still lookin' to get even with both of us, and if you show your face in town, they'll go after you."

"I ain't gonna show my face," Rile said, giving his hat a tug. He had a silly grin that showed he was obviously enjoying the plan he had conceived.

Kenyon sighed and shook his head. "I hope you know what you're doin'. Remember that I asked you not to get involved."

"Yeah, I know," Riley said, still keeping his grin.

Kenyon stuck his hand out. "If I don't make it, you can have everything I've got, horse, gun . . . everything."

Riley shook his head. "I've seen you draw, and I've seen you shoot. In my mind there ain't none better'n you. I figure you could take him without my helpin' you, but don't you worry none. I'll distract him fer you. I'd best be a-findin' me a spot 'fore they're all taken up. See you later." He headed around the outskirts of town toward the Drover Saloon at the far end.

Kenyon watched him ride, and in spite of the tension, he could feel a smile spread across his face. He had grown close to Riley in the several months since they had first met. He liked the Kid's sense of humor and easy-going ways. A glance down the main street caused the smile to disappear. There seemed to be an unusually large number of people standing around, waiting for the shoot-out no doubt.

He eased the line-back around the corner and let it walk slowly in the direction of the Drover. Passing Brownlee's General Store, he saw the owner staring at him through the big front window, and then Brownlee stepped to the door to continue watching him. Ark Fletcher, the undertaker, gave him a nod as Kenyon rode by. The town busybody, Tom Nathan, came out of Dunstan's Hardward Store upon seeing Kenyon and proceeded to walk along the boardwalk, keeping the same pace as Kenyon's gelding. All we need is the preacher and his flock, and we'll have the whole town on the street today, Kenyon thought.

As he approached the Drover Saloon, Kenyon saw one of Ben Terrell's cowhands leaning against the wall; the man suddenly straightened up and stepped to the bat-wing doors. In a moment E. J. Wingate, Hank, Shorty, Ben Terrell, and half a dozen others came out to greet him. All of them were smiling.

Kenyon tugged gently on the reins and the dun stopped. It whinnied and blew noisily as though it were expecting trouble. He patted its neck and glanced quickly at the upper floors of each of the two-storied buildings that braced the street. He thought he saw rifles partially protruding through the curtains on the windows of one of the buildings. He didn't think Terrell would try to guarantee success by having a back-up of extra guns, but if it wasn't Terrell's idea, whose was it? He knew E. J. Windgate wouldn't go for the idea, and he also knew that Riley didn't know anyone he could use to provide extra firepower. It bothered him. He dismounted across the street from the Drover and stepped into the center of the sun-drenched dirt strip that served as the town's main drag.

Shorty let out a high cackle. "Well if it ain't the drifter himself. Come to town to see what a real man looks like, didn't you?"

Kenyon smiled. "You wouldn't make a pimple on a good man's ass, Shorty. Now how could you know a *real* one if you saw him?"

"Why you sonofa. . ." Shorty's move to draw his gun was interrupted by E. J. Wingate's whirling and holding up one finger in front of Shorty's nose.

"Shut up!" Wingate barked. "This is my show, and

you ain't gonna ruin it." Turning back to Kenyon again, he let a cold smile play across his features. "Well, Kenyon, I'm mighty pleased to see that you decided not to hide behind that old woman's skirts. A man should learn to take his lumps standin' on his own two feet."

"Maybe you ought to be tellin' that to Ben Terrell. He's been hidin' behind that lard-ass and that little piece of cow chip standin' next to you there for quite a spell now."

Hank and Shorty stepped forward, both livid with rage.

"I don't take that kind of talk from nobody," Hank snarled.

"Hank! Shorty! Goddammit get back here and shut up. If Wingate misses, you'll have your turn." Terrell's voice boomed up and down the street.

"No chance of that," Wingate said, with a big smile still on his face. "You've got everybody riled except me, Kenyon. Make your move."

He separated himself from the others and stepped into the street. His fingers drummed silently on the sides of his holsters.

Riley moved quickly along the balcony of the hotel on the opposite side of the street from Kenyon. If he could just climb up onto the roof of the next building and get there before they started the gunfight, he could fire a shot from a hidden position, and maybe that would distract Wingate long enough for Kenyon to beat him to the draw. He was pleased with his plan. Just as he stepped up on the balcony railing to raise himself to the roof, the railing gave way with a loud, slow ripping sound and Riley went falling down into the bed of an empty wagon someone had hastily left in the street in a hurried attempt to be a clear of the coming gunfight.

The team that was hooked to the wagon reared up

and whinnied loudly and then bolted in a dead run down the street with a stunned Riley lying in the back.

Kenyon drew and fired at almost the same split second that Wingate did. He felt a red-hot flash of pain as Wingate's bullet tore through the flesh on the side of his neck just above the collarbone.

Wingate staggered back, bumping into Hank before he stopped. He stood looking at Kenyon with a puzzled expression on his face, then slowly sank to the ground and fell face downwards into the dirt. The bloody hole the bullet had torn left no doubt he was dead.

As Hank and Shorty drew their weapons, the rifles that Kenyon thought he had seen behind the curtains suddenly protruded and fired, sending both Hank and Shorty falling to the street, fatally wounded. Ben Terrell and four of his men drew their guns, but when another volley of rifle shots, along with a blast from Kenyon's Colt, downed three of them, including Terrell, the other two dropped their guns and put their hands in the air.

Terrell got to his feet holding a bloody arm. He signaled to Ed Wallace, the sheriff, and nodded toward Kenyon.

"Take him in, Sheriff."

Wallace stepped forward, gun drawn, and spoke. "Drop your gun, cowboy. I'm arresting you for the murder of that man." He indicated Wingate with a flick of the hand. "And for the attempted murder of Mr. Terrell and his men."

"You ain't doin' nothin' of the kind, Sheriff," Helen's voice boomed from the hotel window.

Wallace looked up and saw four other women besides Helen training rifles on him. He laughed. "You think I'm backing down because of you women?"

"You'd better pay attention to them, Sheriff," someone said. "Besides, it ain't just women."

Wallace glanced around, and he could see three men on the other side of the street pointing rifles at him.

"You know as well as we do that Kenyon never murdered anybody. Terrell set the whole thing up by hiring a gunslinger to come in and kill Kenyon. It just turned out that Kenyon was a mite faster than that jaybird, and you ain't arrestin' him because he was," Helen yelled.

"She's right, Sheriff."

The voice belonged to a tall rangy-looking man sporting a handlebar moustache and wearing a star pinned to his vest. He stepped through the crowd.

"I'm U.S. Marshal John Tait from Phoenix. I'll take that gun, Sheriff." He relieved Wallace of his gun and then turned to Kenyon. "I'm sorry I was so late getting here. I was trailing three bank robbers, and they went into Apache country. We had a rough time getting out. I should say *I* had a rough time getting out. They didn't make it."

"But I sent a telegram to the governor saying we didn't need a marshal," Terrell said.

"I ain't been near a telegraph office for quite a spell," Tait answered. "I sure didn't know anything about my trip being canceled. From what I've seen here, it's a good thing I came." Turning his attention once more to Kenyon, he continued speaking.

"You're lucky you managed to kill Wingate. He had quite a reputation as a fast gun." Turning back to Wallace, he pointed the sheriff's own gun at him.

"Okay, Sheriff, let's go. You too," he said, nudging Terrell.

Riley sat up in the wagon and shook his head to clear the fuzziness that clung there. He wondered who was driving him off in such a hurry. When he saw that no one was driving, he jumped up and climbed over the seat to grab the rein's. Then, yanking back on them, he yelled.

"Whoa! Whoa you knotheads! Where in the devil are you goin'?"

He turned the wagon around and headed back toward town. His spirits were low and he felt miserable. "I sure messed things up," he muttered. "Kenyon must be dead, and if he is, it's all my fault. Goin' up against Wingate ain't no fair fight. I was just plannin' on givin' Kenyon the edge. He's saved my hide plenty of times, and all I had to do was fire a shot, but I couldn't even do that right. Now he's prob'bly lyin' there in the street all shot to blue blazes."

Kenyon walked over to Doc Weaver's office, but the doctor wasn't in. Mrs. Weaver explained where he was.

"He's over at the jail taking care of Mr. Terrell and those men of his that got all shot up. I'll bandage that up for you," she said, looking at Kenyon's neck.

When she was through, she refused payment. "I'm no doctor," she said, "just a friendly neighbor helping out."

Kenyon thanked her, then walked back to main street to look for Riley. He spotted Herman Konig and walked over to him.

"That vas a good show, Kenyon. I guess that man won't be slinging guns any more for a living, eh?"

Kenyon grinned. "I guess not. Say, you haven't seen Riley around anywhere have you?"

"He fell off the roof and vas going hell-bent in a wagon the last time I see him."

"That was Riley that created all that noise?"

"Ya. I don't know vat he is doing on the roof, but he didn't do it."

Kenyon took Herman's arm. "You'd better get out of the street. Here he comes now."

Riley guided the team up by the boardwalk and stopped them.

His face broke into a grin when he saw Kenyon. "Boy, am I glad to see you." He jumped down and gave Kenyon a big hug. "I'm sorry I made a mess out of—"

Kenyon knew that Riley was going to apologize for what he had done, so he interrupted Riley in the middle of his speech.

"That distraction you did was perfect. Wingate slowed down and looked to see what the trouble was, and that's when I got him."

Riley looked perplexed. Then a big grin spread across his face once more. "I'm sure glad I helped you out. I was just goin' to say I'm sorry I made a mess out of that balcony up there and then missed all the shootin', but I knew I had to do it."

"You didn't miss much. The two of us put away one of the fastest gunfighters in the country, and Helen and her friends put Shorty and Hank out of action, and the marshal took Terrell to jail."

"Jeeze, and I had to miss it all."

The bartender from the Drover came up to shake Kenyon's hand.

"That was the fastest draw I've ever had the pleasure of seeing. I knew that Wingate was supposed to be one of the best, but you were greased lightning. I'd like to buy you a drink if I may."

Kenyon nodded. "I could use one right about now. How about you, Herman? Riley?"

"Why, heckfire yeah," Riley answered.

"Ya, I have one."

As they walked, the bartender began talking again. "You know that Wingate must have had nerves of steel. When those horses reared up and that wagon took off, he didn't bat an eye. Me, I almost fainted right there on the spot. I noticed you didn't flinch either. I sure don't know how you did it."

Kenyon spoke, hoping that Riley woudn't catch the discrepancy between his statement about how Wingate had reacted to the wagon and the one the bartender just gave.

"Well, I was expecting it and Wingate wasn't. Did you notice how the women joined in and kept Terrell and his men from ganging up?"

"Ya," Herman said. "I vas surprised."

"So were they," the bartender added, laughing.

"I missed the whole danged thing," Riley mumbled as they entered the saloon.

17

HELEN ROUNDED UP HER WIDOW FRIENDS and spoke softly to them as she saw Kenyon and Riley talking on the street.

"I want all of you to stop by your cabins and git them pies and cakes and breads and things you've baked and bring 'em out to my place within' an hour. I invited all them men that showed up with a gun to bring their families and come out fer some sweets and coffee and lemonade and such. I asked Herman Konig to keep Kenyon and Riley busy fer at least an hour to give us time to set up some tables outside. That's why you cain't take too long."

"I've got my bread in the wagon, so I'm goin' on out to Helen's place now," Alpha said. "I'll see you gals later."

Helen stood with her hands on her hips, staring down the trail toward town. "What in tarnation is keepin' them yahoos? Those durned flies'll be packin' them sweets clear to Californy 'fore they git here . . . Well, it's about time!" she said, as the horses and wagons came into view.

When the wagons pulled up, farmers and their families began unloading. Helen and her group walked out to greet them. The children, full of energy and hunger pains, which had descended in full force as soon as the odor and sight of fresh-baked pies and cakes hit them, worked off their exuberance in a game of tag.

Kenyon and Riley rode in alongside Herman's buckboard. Just as they stopped, Doc Weaver came driving up in his buckboard accompanied by his wife.

Helen and all of the widows came running over to give the "boys" a hug and a warm greeting to Doc and Herman. Helen gave a short welcoming speech to everyone and then invited them all to have some food and drink.

Several of the young girls who ranged in age from thirteen to fifteen began to crowd around Riley. They hadn't actually seen his brave deed themselves. They had been kept out of gunshot range by their mothers because of the danger of being hit by a stray bullet, but they heard various versions of it, and each presentation had been embellished more than the one preceding it. Riley was on a cloud from all the adulation. Suddenly little Isabel Baden shoved her way through the group and handed Riley a large piece of cake. She motioned for him to bend down while she whispered a message.

"I looked around 'til I found the biggest piece they was, and I saved it just for you."

Riley gave her a hug. "I reckon that's about the nicest thang anybody's ever done fer me. Thank you very much."

She beamed and held her head high as she went back to find a piece of cake for herself. Her father came over to shake Riley's hand.

"I never did get a chance to thank you proper for helpin' me out the day that little buzzard shot me. I understand you're stayin' here at Miz Tilsbury's. I'm right proud to have you as a friend and neighbor."

"Thank you very much, Mr. Baden. I'm just glad I was able to help out."

Alpha sidled up to Kenyon and kept her voice low.

"I seen a young filly watchin' you, Kenyon. She had a hungry look if you asked me. She was a-keepin' an eye on you like a red-tail hawk does on a field mouse."

"Maybe she just wants me to get her a second helpin' of cake 'cause she's too shy to get it herself."

Alpha laughed. "I don't believe that's what she had in mind, but then you never know. Why don't you get her a piece? That's her over by them children and she's movin' this way. She ought to be here directly."

Kenyon looked in the direction that Alpha had indicated. The brunette moving toward him had a rather plain-looking face. When one of the little boys playing tag grabbed her dress and ran around behind her, she turned to shoo him away. Kenyon could see her fairly heavy bottom.

"Looks like she could sit a saddle pretty well," he said.

Alpha laughed. "But it might give the horse a backache. Is that what you're sayin'?"

Kenyon grinned. "I think I'll go talk to Doc Weaver."

Alpha was still chuckling as he walked away.

Doc had just finished a piece of cake as Kenyon walked up.

"By golly, these women sure know how to bake. That's about the finest piece of cake I think I've ever had," he said.

Mrs. Weaver cleared her throat and glared at Doc.

"Yeah, it's good," Kenyon said. "Say, Doc, those two Hagan brothers you patched up, are they in jail or what's happened to them?"

"Those were the meanest, most ungrateful pair I've ever had the misfortune of treating. They were in jail for tryin' to kidnap Riley, but since Shorty and Hank were both killed, Marshal Tait will probably let them go, since there's nobody to bring charges against them unless Riley has a mind to, of course."

"Are they able to ride now?"

"Well, I guess they're both fit enough to ride, but they'll be hurting for awhile. Men as mean as those two don't seem to mind a little pain. That big one— Zeke I think his name is—has a nice leg wound that should keep him from bending it for awhile. He won't be able to put that foot in a stirrup for a bit, but it won't stop him from riding, if I have him pegged correctly."

"You do," Kenyon said.

When all of the visitors, except Alpha had gone, Kenyon walked up and put an arm around Helen's shoulders.

"Helen, has anyone ever told you that you're one hell of a woman?"

She laughed. "Yeah, they have, but they didn't mean it the same way you do."

Kenyon looked at Alpha. "I feel the same way about you, Alpha. If you weren't already spoken for, I'd be makin' my play, but I know Terrell's got his eye on you, so I'm bowin' out."

Alpha laughed. "Yessir, we hit it off all right. Course I did the hittin' and the love tap was done with a Winchester, but what the heck. You can't have ever'thing."

"You two are really great, though. You're strong, and you care for people, and—"

"You sure can cook," Riley broke in.

They all laughed.

"I guess I'm just tryin' to say I'm glad I know you and thanks for bein' my friends," Kenyon said.

"Well, as long as we're passin' out the thank-you's, I don't reckon any of us would be enjoyin' this here food today if it weren't for you and young Thomas here," Helen said.

"As long as I have you two together, I thought I'd

take this time to say goodbye," Kenyon said, "I'll be leavin' in the mornin'."

"We sure could use a couple men like you two to stay and help us run the ranch," Helen said.

"Ranch?" Kenyon asked.

"Yeah, we've decided to throw ever'thing together into one big spread," Alpha said. "That'll give us over twelve-hundred acres to run a few cows on and maybe grow a couple of ears of corn. You certain you won't stay on?"

"I don't know about Riley here, but I think I'll be movin' on. There's a place in New Mexico I've been wantin' to see. I'll be comin' back through this way next year, though."

"Well," Riley said, eyeing the rest of the chocolate cake, "this is the best food I've ever et. You sure don't git this on the trail, but . . . heckfire . . . I ain't gonna have you leavin' by yourself. What if you was to meet up with another gunslinger? Who would pertect your back?"

"Good point," Kenyon said, grinning. "Well, ladies, I'm kinda bushed. It's been a long day, so I'm gonna say goodnight. Riley, you go ahead and see if you can finish off the rest of that cake. Otherwise Helen's gonna have to throw it to the hogs. We'll be leavin' at first light. Goodnight ladies and once again . . . thanks."

"Just a minute there, young man," Helen said, stepping forward. "You cain't sneak off without me giving you a hug." She embraced Kenyon and kissed him on the cheek. She noticed there was a slight tinge of redness under his dark tanned cheeks. "Goodbye, son, and God bless you."

Kenyon turned and walked out the door.

It was still a little dark out when Kenyon awoke, but the top rim of the mountains to the east wore a mantle of light gray that would soon turn to russet when the sun threw its golden spears into the darkened canyons on the western slopes. He leaned over and gave Riley a nudge. "Reach for your drawers, Riley. I've got you covered."

Riley sat bolt upright, eyes wide open. Then the grogginess began to fade as his brain cleared itself of sleep.

"Whew!" he said, and dropped back on the bed. "You scairt the daylights out of me, Kenyon. That Wingate fella was a-takin' aim at me, and he was just squeezin' off a shot when you woke me up. Boy, I tell you, that was a close one."

"Well, let's get movin' before Helen wakes up. She's gonna be cryin' up a storm if she's awake when we leave, so you're gonna have to move real careful like."

They rolled their blankets around their extra shirts and pants and tied them behind the cantles of their saddles. Then they quietly saddled up and rode down the trail away from the house.

Helen stood at the window watching them go. Then, sniffing loudly, tears streaming down her face, she turned away and headed for the stove to put on a pot of coffee.

"You reckon Miz Tilsbury and them other women will be okay without some menfolk like us around?" Riley asked.

Kenyon smiled. "They seemed to have managed for many years without our help. I think they'll do just fine."

"How about us? You thank we'll have them Hagans on our trail anymore?"

Kenyon glanced at Riley who was looking back over his shoulder to see if they were being followed. "Kid, I've seen you stay as cool as a mountain stream when we were up against the best gunfighter in these parts. You don't have to worry about the Hagans anymore. We're a match for the best of them."

Riley grinned. "Yeah . . . I reckon we are."

He took a final look at the valley as they crested a ridge. He had some exciting times there, but being with Kenyon would beat anything the valley had to offer. He nudged the pinto to catch up. It was going to be another fine day.